PAUL CAIN SEVEN SLAYERS

Paul Cain is a pseudonym for George Carroll
Syms, who was born in Des Moines, Iowa, in
1902. He wrote screenplays under the name of
Peter Ruric. He is the author of one novel, *Fast
One,* and one short-story collection, *Seven
Slayers.*

BOOKS BY PAUL CAIN

Fast One
Seven Slayers

SEVEN SLAYERS

PAUL CAIN

VINTAGE CRIME / BLACK LIZARD
VINTAGE BOOKS · A DIVISION OF RANDOM HOUSE, INC. · NEW YORK

First Vintage Crime / Black Lizard Edition, April 1994

ISBN 0-679-75185-8
LC Number: 87-70576

Manufactured in the United States of America
10 9 8 7 6 5 4 3 2 1

CONTENTS

SEVEN SLAYERS

The man said: "McCary."

"No." I shook my head and started to push past him, and he said: "McCary," again thickly, and then he crumpled into a heap on the wet sidewalk.

It was dark there, there wasn't anyone on the street—I could have walked away. I started to walk away and then the sucker instinct got the best of me and I went back and bent over him.

I shook him and said: "Come on, chump—get up out of the puddle."

A cab came around the corner and its headlights shone on me—and there I was, stooping over a drunk whom I'd never seen before, who thought my name was McCary. Any big-town driver would have pegged it for a stick-up, would have shoved off or sat still. That wasn't a big town—the cab slid alongside the curb and a fresh-faced kid stuck his face into the light from the meter and said: "Where to?"

I said: "No place." I ducked my head at the man on the sidewalk. "Maybe this one'll ride—he's paralyzed."

The kid clucked: "Tch, tch."

He opened the door and I stooped over and took hold of the drunk under his armpits and jerked him up and across the sidewalk and into the cab. He was heavy in a funny limp way. There was a hard bulge on his left side, under the arm.

I had an idea. I asked the kid: "Who's McCary?"

He looked self-consciously blank for a minute and then he said: "There's two—Luke and Ben. Luke's the old man—owns a lot of real estate. Ben runs a pool-hall."

"Let's go see Ben," I said. I got into the cab.

We went several blocks down the dark street and then I tapped on the glass and motioned to the kid to pull over to the curb. He stopped and slid the glass and I said: "Who's McCary?"

1

"I told you."

I said: "What about him?"

The kid made the kind of movement with his shoulders that would pass for a shrug in the sticks. "I told you—he runs a pool-hall."

I said: "Listen. This guy came up to me a few minutes ago and said 'McCary'—this guy is very dead."

The kid looked like he was going to jump out of the cab. His eyes were hanging out.

I waited.

The kid swallowed. He said: "Let's dump him."

I shook my head slightly and waited.

"Ben and the old man don't get along—they've been raising hell the last couple of weeks. This is the fourth." He jerked his head towards the corpse beside me.

"Know him?"

He shook his head and then—to be sure—took a flashlight out of the side-pocket and stuck it back through the opening and looked at the man's dead face. He shook his head again.

I said: "Let's go see Ben."

"You're crazy, Mister. If this is one of Ben's boys he'll tie you up to it, and if it ain't . . ."

"Let's go see Ben."

Ben McCary was a blond fat man, about forty—he smiled a great deal.

We sat in a little office above his pool-hall and he smiled heartily across all his face and said: "Well, sir—what can I do for you?"

"My name is Black. I came over from St. Paul—got in about a half hour ago."

He nodded, still with the wide hearty smile; stared at me cordially out of his wide-set blue eyes.

I went on: "I heard there was a lot of noise over here and I thought I might make a connection—pick up some change."

McCary juggled his big facial muscles into something resembling innocence.

"I don't know just what you mean, Buddy," he said. "What's your best game?"

"What's yours?"

2

He grinned again. "Well," he said, "you can get plenty of action up in the front room."

I said: "Don't kid me, Mister McCary. I didn't come over here to play marbles."

He looked pleasantly blank.

"I used to work for Dickie Johnson down in K C," I went on.

"Who sent you to me?"

"Man named Lowry—that's the name on the label of his coat. He's dead."

McCary moved a little in his chair but didn't change his expression.

"I came in on the nine-fifty train," I went on, "and started walking uptown to a hotel. Lowry came up to me over on Dell Street and said 'McCary,' and fell down. He's outside in a cab—stiff."

McCary looked up at the ceiling and then down at the desk. He said: "Well, well"—and took a skinny little cigar out of a box in one of the desk-drawers and lighted it. He finally got around to looking at me again and said: "Well, well," again.

I didn't say anything.

After he'd got the cigar going, he turned another of his big smiles on and said: "How am I supposed to know you're on the level?"

I said: "I'll bite. What do *you* think?"

He laughed. "I like you," he said. "By——! I like you."

I said I thought that was fine and, "Now let's try to do some business."

"Listen," he said. "Luke McCary has run this town for thirty years. He ain't my old man—he married my mother and insisted on my taking his name."

He puffed slowly at his cigar. "I guess I was a pretty ornery kid"—he smiled boyishly—"when I came home from school I got into a jam—you know—kid stuff. The old man kicked me out."

I lighted a cigarette and leaned back.

"I went down to South America for about ten years, and then I went to Europe. I came back here two years ago and everything was all right for a while and then the old man and I got to scrapping again."

I nodded.

"He'd had everything his own way too long. I opened this place about three months ago and took a lot of his gambling business away—a lot of the shipyard men and miners. . . ."

McCary paused, sucked noisily at his cigar.

"Luke went clean off his nut," he went on. "He thought I was going to take it all away from him. . . ." McCary brought his big fist down hard on the desk. "And by the ——! I *am*. Lowry's the third man of mine in two weeks. It's plenty in the open now."

I said: "How about Luke's side?"

"We got one of the——" he said. "A runner."

"It isn't entirely over the gambling concession?"

"Hell, no. That's all it was at first. All I wanted was to make a living. Now I've got two notch-joints at the other end of town. I've got a swell protection in with the law and I'm building up a liquor business that would knock your eye out."

I asked: "Is Luke in it by himself?"

McCary shook his head slowly. "He don't show anywhere. There's a fellah named Stokes runs the works for him—a young fellah. They been partners nearly eight years. It's all in Stokes' name. . . ."

"What does Stokes look like?"

"Tall—about your build. Shiny black hair, and a couple of big gold teeth"—McCary tapped his upper front teeth with a fat finger—"here."

I said: "How much is he worth to you?"

McCary stood up. He leaned across the desk and grinned down at me and said: "Not a nickel." His eyes were wide and clear like a baby's. He said slowly: "The old man is worth twenty-five hundred smackers to *you*."

I didn't say anything and McCary sat down and opened another drawer and took out a bottle of whiskey. He poured a couple of drinks.

"I think the best angle for you," he said, "is to go to Stokes and give him the same proposition you gave me. Nobody saw you come in here. It's the only way you can get near the old man."

I nodded. We drank.

4

"By——! I like your style," he said. "I've been trying to get along with an outfit of yokels."

We smiled at one another. I was glad he said he liked me because I knew he didn't like me at all. I was one up on him, I didn't like him very well either.

Stokes sat on a corner of the big library-table, his long legs dangling.

He said: "You're airing Ben—how do we know you'll play ball with us?" His eyes were stony.

I looked at the old man. I said: "I don't like that fat—son of yours—and I never double-cross the best offer."

Luke McCary was a thin little man with a pinched red face, bushy white hair. He sat in a big armchair on the other side of the table, his head and neck and wild white hair sticking up out of the folds of a heavy blue bathrobe.

He looked at me sharply. He said: "I don't want any part of it."

"Then I'll have to act on the best offer."

Stokes grinned.

The old man stood up. He said: "Why—damn you and your guts. . . ." He opened a humidor on the table and took out a small automatic. "I can shoot the buttons off your vest, young fella . . . I can shoot you for a yegg right now, and no one'll ever know the difference. . . ."

I said: "*You'll* know the difference—for not having taken advantage of talent, when you had the chance."

He put the automatic back in the box and sat down and smiled gently at Stokes.

Stokes was looking at the floor. He said: "Five grand if you wipe out the whole outfit. Run 'em out of town, stick 'em in jail, poison 'em . . . Anything."

"Wouldn't you like a new railroad station too?"

They didn't say anything for a minute. They looked at me.

I went on: "No sale. I'll take care of Ben for that—but busting up the organization would mean sending for a few friends—would cost a hell of a lot more than five. . . ."

The old man looked the least bit scared for a second—then he said: "Ben'll do."

5

"How about laying something on the line?"

Stokes said: "Don't be silly."

The old man cackled. "Well I never saw such guts," he said.

I said: "All right, gentlemen. Maybe I'll call you later."

Stokes went downstairs with me. He smiled in a strange way. "I never knew the old man to go for anything that looks as tricky as this. I guess it looks good because Ben thinks you're working for him."

I nodded. I said: "Uh huh—Ben's a swell guy. He'll probably blast me on sight."

"I don't think you'll find him at his joint."

I waited and Stokes leaned against the door, said: "There's a big outfit downstate that's been running twelve trucks a week through here from the Border. They've paid off for this division of the highway for years—to the old man. The last two convoys have been hi-jacked at Four-mile Creek, north of town—a couple drivers were killed. . . ."

He paused, looked wise a minute, went on: "That was Ben. There was a convoy due through last night—they run in bunches of four, or six—it didn't show up. It's a cinch for tonight—and that's where Ben'll be."

I said: "That's fine. How do I get there?"

Stokes told me to follow the main highway north, and where to take the cutoff that crossed Four-mile. I thanked him and went out.

I walked down to a drugstore on the corner and called a cab. When it came, I got in and had the driver jockey around until he was parked in a spot where I could watch the front door of the McCary house.

After a while, Stokes came out and got into a roadster and snorted up past us and turned down the side street. I told the driver to follow him. I don't think the driver knew who it was. It didn't matter a hell of a lot anyway.

I got out and told the driver to wait and walked on down Dell Street, keeping close to the fence. It was raining pretty hard again. I passed the place where Lowry had come up to me, and I went on to the corner; and then went back the same way until I came to the narrow gate I had missed in the darkness.

6

It was more a door than a gate, set flush with the high fence. I finagled with the latch for a while and then pushed the gate open slowly and went into a yard. It was a big yard, full of old lumber and old box-car trucks—stuff like that. There was a long shed along one side, and a small two-story building on the far side.

I stumbled along as quietly as I could towards the building and then I went around the corner of a big pile of ties, and Stokes' roadster was sitting there very dark and quiet in the rain. I went past it and up to the building and along the wall until I saw the lighted window.

I had to rustle around quietly and find a box and stand on it to see through the little square window. The panes were dirty; the inside looked like a time-office. Stokes and Ben McCary and another man were there. They were arguing about something. McCary was walking around waving his arms; Stokes and the other man were sitting down. I couldn't hear a word they said. The rain was roaring on the tin-roof of the shed and all I could hear was a buzz of voices.

I didn't stay there very long. It didn't mean anything. I got down and put the box back and wandered around until I found McCary's car. Anyway, I guessed it was his car. It was a big touring-car and it was parked near the gate on the opposite side of the block from Dell Street, where Stokes had come in.

I got in and sat in the back seat. The side-curtains were drawn and it was nice to get out of the rain for a while.

In about ten minutes, the light went out and I could hear voices coming towards the car. I sat down on the floor. The three of them stood outside for a minute talking about "a call from Harry"—then Stokes and the other man went off towards Stokes' car, and McCary squeezed into the front seat and stepped on the starter.

I waited till we had burned through the gate and were halfway up the block, and then I put a gun against the back of McCary's neck. He straightened out in the seat and eased the brake on. I told him to go on to the old man's house.

We sat in the big room upstairs. The old man sat in the big armchair by the table, and Ben sat across from him. I was half lying down in another chair out of the circle of light and I had the gun on my lap.

The old man was fit to be tied. He was green with hate and he kept glaring at Ben out of his little red-rimmed eyes.

I said: "Well, gran'pa—if you'll make out that check now, we'll finish this business."

The old man swallowed.

"You can give me *your* twenty-five hundred in cash," I went on to Ben. "Then I'll put the chill on both of you—and everybody'll be happy."

They must have thought I meant it. Ben got rigid, and the old man cleared his throat and made a slow pass at the humidor.

I fiddled with the gun. I threw a pack of cigarettes on the table and said: "Smoke?"

The old man looked at the cigarettes and at the gun in my hand, and relaxed.

I said: "Still and all—it don't quite square with my weakness for efficiency, yet. Maybe you boys'll get together and make me an offer for Stokes. He's the star—he's been framing both of you."

I don't think Ben was very surprised—but the old man looked like he'd swallowed a mouse.

"He's been in with Ben on the truck heistings," I went on. "He's been waiting for a good spot to dump you—working on your connections."

The old man said: "That's a——damned lie."

"Suit yourself."

I went on to Ben: "He made the five-grand offer for your hide, in Luke's name, tonight—and he gave me the Four-mile steer. . . ." I hesitated a moment. "Only you wouldn't try three in the same spot, would you?"

Ben finally got his smile working. He started to say something but I interrupted him:

"Stokes told me you rubbed the two boys on the trucks, too."

Ben's smile went out like a light. He said: "Stokes shot both those men himself—and there wasn't any need for it. They were lined up alongside the road. . . ."

Something in the soft way he said it made it sound good.

I said: "He'll be around your place—no?"

8

"He went home."

Ben gave me the number and I called up, but there wasn't any answer.

We sat there without saying anything for several minutes, and then the door downstairs opened and closed and somebody came up.

I said to Ben: "What'll you bet?"

The door opened and Stokes came in. He had a long gray raincoat on and it made him look even taller and thinner than he was. He stood in the doorway looking mostly at the old man; then he came in and sat down on a corner of the table.

I said: "Now that the class is all here, you can start bidding."

The old man laughed deep in his throat. Stokes was watching me expressionlessly, and Ben sat smiling stupidly at his hands.

"I'm auctioning off the best little town in the state, gentlemen," I went on. "Best schools, sewage system, post-office. . . . Best street-lighting, water supply. . . ."

I was having a swell time.

The old man was staring malevolently at Stokes. "I'll give you twenty-five thousand dollars," he said to me, "to give me that pistol and get out of here."

If I'd thought there was any chance of collecting, I might have talked to him. Things happen that way sometimes.

I looked at my watch and put the gun down on the arm of the chair where it looked best and picked up the phone.

I asked Ben: "Where's the business going to be pulled off tonight?"

Ben wanted to be nice. He said: "A coffee joint about six miles north of town." He glanced at Stokes. "This——tried to swing it back to Four-mile when he thought you'd be there sniping for me."

"The boys are there now?"

He nodded. "The trucks have been stopping there to eat lately."

I asked the operator for long-distance, and asked for the Bristol Hotel in Talley, the first town north. The connection went right through. I asked for Mister Cobb.

When he answered, I told him about the coffee place, and

that I wasn't sure about it; and told him he'd find the stuff that had been heisted in the sheds of the yard on Dell Street. I wasn't sure of that either, but I watched Ben and Stokes when I said it and it looked all right. Cobb told me that he'd gotten into Talley with the convoy about midnight and had been waiting for my call since then.

I hung up. "There'll be some swell fireworks out there," I said. "There's a sub-machine-gun on every truck—double crews. And it don't matter much," I went on to Ben, "how good your steer is. They'll be watching out all the way."

Stokes stood up.

I picked up the gun. "Don't move so far, Skinny," I said. "It makes me nervous."

He stood there staring at the gun. The water was running off his raincoat and it had formed into a little dark pool at his feet.

He said: "What the hell do you want?"

"I wanted you to know that one of the kids you shot up last week at Four-mile was my boss' brother. He went along for the ride."

I don't think Stokes could move. I think he tried to move sidewise or get his hand into his pocket, or something, but all he could do was take a deep breath. Then I shot him in the middle of the body where he shot the kid, and he sank down on the floor with his legs crossed under him, like a tailor.

The old man didn't get up. He sat a little deeper in his chair and stared at Stokes.

Ben moved very fast for a fat man. He was up and out the door like a bat out of hell. That was OK with me—he couldn't get to the coffee place before the trucks got there. I had the keys to his car, and it was too far anyway.

I got up and put the rod away and went over to the table and picked up my cigarettes. I looked down at the old man, said: "Things'll be a little quieter now, maybe. You'll get the dough for haulage through your territory, as usual. See that it gets through."

He didn't answer.

I started for the door and then there was a shot out in front of the house. I ran on down to the front door. It was open and Ben was flat on the threshold—had fallen smack on his face, half through the door.

I ducked back through the hall and tried a couple locked doors. When I came up through the hall again, the old man was on his knees beside Ben, and was rocking back and forth, moaning a little.

I went through another room and into the kitchen and on through, out the back door. I crossed the backyard and jumped a low fence and walked through another yard to a gate that led into an alley. I sloshed along through the mud until I came to a cross-street, and went on down to the corner that was diagonally across the block from the McCary house.

A cab came down the street and I waited until it was almost to the corner, stepped out in front of it. The driver swerved and stepped on the gas, but he had slowed enough to give me time to jump on the running-board.

I stuck my head in to the light from the meter. That turned out to be my best hunch of the evening because in another second, the driver would have opened up my chest with one of the dirtiest looking .45's I ever saw, at about two feet. It was the kid who had picked Lowry and me up. He hesitated just long enough when he saw who I was.

We nearly ran into a tree and I had time to reach in and knock that cannon out of his hand. He stepped on the brake, and reached for the gun, but I beat him to it by a hair and stuck it in my overcoat pocket and got in beside him.

I said: "Shame on you—almost crashing an old pal like me."

He sat tight in the seat and got a weak grin working and said: "Where to?"

"Just away."

We went on through the mud and rain, and turned into a slightly better lighted street.

I said: "How did you know Ben shot Lowry?"

The kid kept his head down, his eyes ahead. "Lowry and me have lived together for two years," he said. "He used to be in the hack racket too, till he got mixed up with McCary. . . .

"Lowry won a lot of jack in one of Ben's crap games a couple day ago, and Ben wanted him to kick back with it—said everybody that worked for him was automatically a shill, and couldn't play for keeps. But Lowry's been

11

dropping every nickel he made in the same game, for months. That was okay with Ben. It was all right to lose, but you mustn't win."

I nodded, lighted a cigarette.

"Ben shot Lowry tonight at the joint on Dell Street. I know it was him because Lowry's been afraid of it—and that's why he said 'McCary.'"

"Did you know it was Lowry when you picked us up?"

"Not until I used the light. Then, when we got to Ben's I saw him get out of his car and go in just ahead of you—then I was sure. I took Lowry up to his pa's after you went in."

The kid drove me to the next town south. I forget the name. I got a break on a train—I only had to wait about ten minutes.

Shane pressed the button beneath the neat red 71. Then he leaned close against the building and tilted his head a little and looked up at the thick yellow-black sky. Rain swept in great uneven and diagonal sheets across the dark street, churned the dark puddle at his feet. The street-light at the corner swung, creaked in the wind.

Light came suddenly through a slit in the door, the door was opened. Shane went into a narrow heavily carpeted hallway. He took off his dark soft hat, shook it back and forth, handed it to the man who had opened the door.

He said: "Hi, Nick. How is it?"

Nick said: "It is very bad weather—and business is very bad."

Nick was short, very broad. It was not fat broadness, but muscled, powerful. His shoulders sloped heavily to long curving arms, big white hands. His neck was thick and white and his face was broad and so white that his long black hair looked like a cap. He hung Shane's hat on one of a long row of numbered pegs, helped him with his coat, hung it beside the hat.

He stared at Shane reproachfully. "He has been waiting for you a long time," he said.

Shane said: "Uh-huh," absently, went back along the hallway and up a flight of narrow stairs. At the top he turned into another hallway, crossed it diagonally to an open double doorway.

The room was large, dimly lighted. Perhaps fifteen or eighteen people, mostly in twos or threes, sat at certain of the little round white covered tables. Three more, a woman and two men, stood at the aluminum bar that ran across one corner.

Shane stood in the doorway a moment, then crossed the room to where Rigas sat waiting for him at a table against the far wall. Several people looked up, nodded or spoke as he passed; he sat down across the table from Rigas, said: "Bacardi," to the hovering waiter.

Rigas folded his paper, leaned forward with his elbows on the table and smiled.

"You are late, my friend." He put up one hand and rubbed one side of his pale blue jaw.

Shane nodded slightly. He said: "I've been pretty busy."

Rigas was Greek. His long rectangular face was deeply lined; his eyes were small, dark, wide-set; his mouth was a pale upward-curved gash. He was in dinner clothes.

He said: "Things are good with you— Yes?"

Shane shrugged. "Fair."

"Things are very bad here." Rigas picked up his cocktail, sipped it, leaned back.

Shane waited.

"Very bad," Rigas went on. "They have raised our protection overhead more than fifty per cent."

The waiter lifted Shane's cocktail from the tray with a broad flourish, put it on the table in front of him. Shane looked at it, then up at Rigas, said: "Well. . . ."

Rigas was silent. He stared at the tablecloth, with his thin lips stuck out in an expression of deep concentration.

Shane tasted his cocktail, laughed a little. "You know damned well," he said, "that I'm not going to put another dime into this place." He put down his glass and stared morosely at Rigas. "And you know that I can't do anything about your protection arrangement. That's your business."

Rigas nodded sadly without looking up. "I know—I know."

Shane sipped his drink, waited.

Rigas finally looked up, spoke hesitantly: "Lorain— Lorain is going to get a divorce."

Shane smiled, said: "That's a break."

Rigas nodded slowly. "Yes." He spoke very slowly, deliberately: "Yes—that is a break for all of us."

Shane leaned forward, put his elbows on the table, put one hand down slowly, palm up. He stared at Rigas and his face was hard, his eyes were very cold. He said: "You made that kind of a crack once before—remember?"

14

Rigas didn't speak. He gazed wide-eyed, expression-lessly at Shane's tie.

"Remember what happened?" Shane went on.

Rigas didn't speak, or move.

Shane relaxed suddenly. He leaned back, glanced around, smiled faintly.

"I back this joint," he said, "because I thought you might make it go. I don't like you—never have—but I like Lorain, have liked her ever since we were kids together. I thought she was an awful chump when she married you and I told her so."

He sipped his cocktail, widened his smile. "She told me what a great guy you were," he went on, "an' she stuck to it, even after you'd dropped all your dough, and hers. Then she told me you wanted to take over this place, an' I came in on it, laid fifteen grand on the line."

Rigas moved uncomfortably in his chair, glanced swiftly around the room.

"Since then," Shane went on, "I've chunked in some-where around five more. . . ."

Rigas interrupted: "We've got nearly twelve thousand dollars' worth of stock." He made a wide gesture.

"What for?" Shane curved his mouth to a pleasant sneer. "So you can be knocked over, and keep the enforcement boys in vintage wines for a couple of months."

Rigas shrugged elaborately, turned half away. "I cannot talk to you," he said. "You fly off the handle. . . ."

"No." Shane smiled. "You can talk to me all you like, Charley—and I don't fly off the handle—and I'm not squawking. But don't make any more cracks about Lorain and me. Whatever I've done for you I've done for her—because I like her. Like her. Can you get that through that thick spick skull of yours? I wouldn't want her if she was a dime a dozen—an' I don't like that raised eyebrow stuff. It sounds like pimp."

Rigas' face turned dull red. His eyes were very sharp and bright. He stood up, spoke very softly, breathlessly, as if it was hard for him to get all the words out: "Let's go upstairs, Dick."

Shane got up and they crossed the room together, went out through the double door.

15

On the third floor they crossed an identical hallway, Rigas unlocked a tall gray door and they went into another large room. There were two large round tables, each with a green-shaded drop-light over it. There were eight men at one of the tables, seven at the other; Rigas and Shane crossed the room to another tall gray door.

The stud dealer and two players looked up from the nearest table, one of the players said: "H' are yah, Charley?" Then Rigas opened the tall door and they went into a little room that was furnished as an office.

Rigas pressed the light switch, closed the door and stood with his back to it for a moment. His hands were in his coat pockets.

Shane sat down on the edge of the desk.

Rigas crossed to the desk slowly and when he was near Shane he jerked his right hand out of his pocket suddenly and swung a thin-bladed knife up at Shane's throat.

Shane moved a little to one side, grabbed Rigas' arm near the elbow with one open hand; the knife ripped up crosswise across the lapel of his coat. At the same time he brought his right knee up hard against Rigas' stomach. Rigas grunted and one of his knees gave way and he slumped down slowly, sidewise to the floor. The knife clattered on the glass desk-top.

As Shane slid off the desk, stood over Rigas, the door opened and a very tall, very spare man came a little way into the room.

Shane glanced at the man and then he looked down at Rigas and his eyes were almost closed, his mouth was a thin hard line. Rigas groaned and held his hands tight against his stomach, his chin tight against his chest.

Shane looked up at the tall man, said: "You'd better not let this brother of yours play with knives. He's liable to put somebody's eye out." He spoke with his teeth together.

The tall man stared blankly at Rigas.

Shane went past the tall man, to the door, went out and across the big room. All of the men at the tables were looking at him; all of them were very quiet. Two men were standing up at the nearest table.

Shane went out and closed the door behind him, went swiftly down two flights. He found his hat and coat and put

16

them on. Nick came up from the basement as he was knotting his scarf.

Nick said: "Shall I get you a cab, Mister Shane?"

Shane shook his head. He slid the big bolt and opened the door and went out into the driving rain. He walked to Madison Avenue, got into a cab and said: "Valmouth—on Forty-Ninth."

It was five minutes after eight.

Shane's rooms at the Valmouth were on the eighteenth floor. He stood at one of the wide windows and looked down through the swirling, beating rain to Fiftieth Street.

After a little while he went into the bathroom, turned off the water that was roaring into the tub, slipped off his robe.

Someone knocked at the outer door and he called: "Come in," looked into the long mirror in the bathroom door that reflected part of the living room. A waiter with a wide oval tray opened the door, came in and put the tray down on a low table.

Shane said: "There's some change on the telephone stand." He kicked off his slippers and stepped into the tub.

In five minutes he was out, had put on a long dark-green robe, slippers, and was sitting at the low table cutting a thick T-bone steak into dark pink squares.

As he poured coffee the phone buzzed; he leaned sidewise, picked it up, said: "Hello." Then he said: "Mister Shane is not in. . . . She's on the way up! . . . What the hell did you let her start up for? . . ."

He slammed the phone down, went swiftly to the door and turned the bolt. He stood near the door a moment, then shrugged slightly, turned the bolt back and went slowly back and sat down.

Lorain Rigas was slender, dark. Her black eyes slanted upward a little at the corners, her mouth was full, deeply red, generous. She wore a dark close-fitting raincoat, a small suede hat. She closed the door and stood with her back to it.

Shane said: "Coffee?"

She shook her head. She said: "Charley called me up this afternoon and said he was going to give me the divorce— that he wouldn't fight it."

17

"That's fine." Shane put two lumps of sugar in a spoon, held it in the coffee and intently watched the sugar crumble, disappear. "So what?"

She came over and sat down near him. She unbuttoned her coat, crossed her slim silken legs, took a cigarette out of a tiny silver case and lighted it.

She said: "So you've got to help me locate Del before he gets to Charley."

Shane sipped his coffee, waited.

"Del started drinking last night," she went on, "an' he kept it up this morning. He went out about eleven, and some time around one, Jack Kenny called up an' told me that Del was over at his joint—roaring drunk, and howling for Charley's blood. He gets that way every time he gets boiled—crazy jealous about Charley and me."

She leaned back and blew a thin cone of smoke at the ceiling. "I told Jack to let him drink himself under the table, or lock him up, or something—an' in a little while Jack called back and said everything was all right—that Del had passed out."

Shane was smiling a little. He got up and went to the central table and took a long green-black cigar from a humidor, clipped it, lighted it. Then he went back and sat down.

The girl leaned forward. "About three o'clock," she said, "the Eastman Agency—that's the outfit I've had tailing Charley for evidence—called up and said they'd located the apartment house up on the West Side where Charley's been living with the McLean woman. . . ."

Shane said: "How long have they been on the case?"

"Three days—an' Charley's ducked them until today—they traced a phone call or something."

Shane nodded, poured more coffee into the little cup.

Lorain Rigas mashed out her cigarette. "I told Eastman to keep his boys on the apartment until they spotted Charley going in—then I figured on going over tonight and crashing in with a load of witnesses—but in a little while Charley calls me and says everything's okay, that he'll give me the divorce any time, any place, and so on."

Shane said: "You've had a busy day."

"Uh-huh." She reached over and picked up the cup of coffee, sipped a little. "I didn't call Eastman back—I figure on going through with it the way I intended to—get the evidence an' the affidavits an' what not. Then if Charley changes his mind. . . ." She put the cup back on the tray, leaned back and lighted another cigarette. "But we've got to find Del."

Shane said: "I thought he was cold at Kenny's."

She shook her head, smiled. "I called Kenny to see how Del was, and Del was gone. He came to and started where he left off—stole a gun out of Jack's trunk, and went out the back way. I don't think he'd really go through with it, but he goes nuts when he gets enough red-eye under his belt. . . ."

Shane was leaning far back in the deep chair, staring vacantly at the ceiling. He said: "If you think Del would really make a pass at Charley—" He puffed at the cigar, finished slowly: "You don't seem quite as excited about it as you should be."

"What the hell's the use getting excited?" She stood up. "It's a cinch they won't let Del into 71—an' he wouldn't wait outside for Charley—not when he's drunk. He gets big ideas about face to face and man to man when he's drunk. I know Del."

"Then what are you worrying about?" Shane looked up at her, smiled gently. "He's probably at home waiting for you."

"No—I just called up." She went over to the window.

Shane looked at her back. He said: "You're pretty crazy about Del—aren't you?"

She nodded without turning.

Shane put his cigar down, reached for the phone. "Where do you think we ought to start?"

She turned, cocked her head a little to one side and looked at him sleepily. "If I knew where we ought to start, Dick," she said, "I wouldn't have had to bother you. You've known Del for years—you know the screwy way his mind works as well as I do—and you know the places. Where would he go, do you think, looking for Charley—besides 71?"

Shane picked up the phone, stared at it a little while, put it down. He got up, said: "I'm going to put on some clothes," and went into the bedroom.

19

Lorain Rigas sat down near the window. She pushed the small suede hat back off her forehead, leaned back and closed her eyes.

When Shane came in, knotting his tie, she was lying very still. He stood over her a moment, looking out the window. Then he finished his tie and looked down at her and put one hand out tentatively, touched her forehead with his fingers. She opened her eyes and looked up at him expressionlessly for a little while; he turned and went to the chair where he had thrown his coat, put it on.

The phone buzzed a second after Shane had closed and locked the door. He swore under his breath, fished in his pockets. The girl leaned against the wall of the corridor, smiled at his futile efforts to find the key.

The phone buzzed insistently.

He finally found the key, unlocked the door hurriedly, and went to the phone. Lorain Rigas leaned against the frame of the open door.

Shane said: "Hello. . . . Put him on. . . ." He stood, holding the phone, looking at the girl; spoke again into the phone: "Hello, Bill. . . . Yeah. . . . Yeah. . . . What the hell for . . . ?" Then he was silent a while with the receiver at his ear. Finally he said: "Okay, Bill—thanks." Hung up slowly.

He sat down, gestured with his head for the girl to come in and close the door. She closed the door and stood with her back to it, staring at him questioningly.

He said: "Charley was shot to death in the Montecito Apartments on West Eighty-Second, some time around eight-thirty tonight."

Lorain Rigas put her hand out slowly, blindly a little way. Her eyes were entirely blank. She went slowly, unsteadily to a chair, sank into it.

Shane said: "They're holding the McLean gal—an' they've found out that Charley and I had an argument this evening—they want to talk to me. They're on the way over to pick me up."

He glanced at his watch. It was nine-forty. He got up and went to the table, took a cigar from the humidor, lighted it. Then he went to the window and stared out into the darkness.

* * * * *

"One—base of brain. One—slightly lower—shattered cervical." The autopsy surgeon straightened, tossed the glittering instrument into a sterilizer and skinned off his rubber gloves. He glanced at Shane, turned and started towards the door.

Sergeant Gill and an intern turned the body over.

Gill said: "Rigas?" looked up at Shane.

Shane nodded.

Gill spread a partially filled-out form on the examining table near Rigas' feet, took a stub of pencil from his pocket and added several lines to the form. Then he folded it and put it in his pocket and said: "Let's go back upstairs."

Shane followed him out of the room that smelled of ether and of death; they went down a long corridor to an elevator.

On the third floor they left the elevator and crossed the hall diagonally to the open door of a large office, went in. A tall, paunched man with a bony, purplish face turned from the window, went to a swivel chair behind the broad desk and sat down.

He said: "How come you stopped by tonight, Dick?" He leaned back, squinted across the desk at Shane.

Shane shrugged, sat down sidewise on the edge of the desk. "Wanted to say hello to all my buddies."

"You're a damned liar!" The tall man spoke quietly, impersonally. "A couple of my men were on the way over to pick you up when you showed up, here. You were tipped, an' I want to know who it was—it don't make so much difference about you, but that kind of thing is bad for the department."

Shane was smiling at Gill. He turned his head to look down at the tall man silently. Finally he said: "What are you going to do, Ed—hold me?"

The tall man said: "Who tipped you to the pinch?"

Shane stood up, faced the tall man squarely. He said: "So it's a pinch?" He turned and started towards the door, spoke over his shoulder to Gill: "Come on, Sarge."

"Come here, you——!"

Shane turned. His expression was not pleasant. He took two short, slow steps back towards the desk.

21

The tall man was grinning. He drawled: "You're hard to get along with—ain't you!"

Shane didn't answer. He stood with one foot a little in advance of the other and stared at the tall man from under the brim of his dark soft hat. The flesh around his eyes and mouth was very tightly drawn.

The tall man moved his grin from Shane to Gill. He said: "See if you can find that Eastman Op."

Gill went out of the room hurriedly.

The tall man swung a little in the chair, turned his head to look out the window. His manner when he spoke was casual, forced:

"The McLean girl killed Rigas."

Shane did not move or speak.

"What did you and him fight about tonight?" The tall man turned to look at Shane. His hands were folded over his broad stomach and he clicked his thumbnails nervously.

Shane cleared his throat. He said huskily: "Am I under arrest?"

"No. But we've got enough to held you on suspicion. You've sunk a lot of dough in Rigas' joint and so far as we know you ain't taken much out. Tonight you had an argument . . ."

The tall man unclasped his hands and leaned forward, put his arms on the desk. "Why don't you help us get this thing right instead of being so damned fidgety?" He twisted his darkly florid face to a wry smile.

Shane said: "Rigas and I had an argument about money—I left his place at eight o'clock and I was in my hotel at a quarter after. I was there until I came here." He went forward again to the desk. "I can get a half-dozen people at the hotel to swear to that."

The tall man made a wide and elaborate gesture of deprecation. "Hell, Dick, we know you didn't do it—and it's almost a natural for McLean. Only we thought you might help us clean up the loose ends."

Shane shook his head slowly, emphatically.

Sergeant Gill came in with an undersized blond youth in a shiny blue-serge suit.

The young man went to the desk, nodded at Shane, said: "H' are you, Cap?" to the tall man.

The tall man was looking at Shane. He said: "This man"—he jerked his head at the youth—"works for Eastman. He was on an evidence job for Mrs. Rigas and went in with the patrolman when Rigas was shot. . . ."

"Yes, sir," the youth interrupted. "The telephone operator come running out screaming bloody murder an' the copper come running down from the corner an' we both went upstairs"—he paused, caught his breath—"an' there was this guy Rigas, half in the bedroom and half out, an' dead as a doornail. . . . The gun was on the floor, and this dame, McLean, was in pyjamas, yelling that she didn't do it."

The tall man said: "Yes—you told us all that before."

"I know—only I'm telling him." The youth smiled at Shane.

Shane sat down again on the edge of the desk. He looked from the youth to the tall man, asked: "What does McLean say?"

"She's got a whole raft of stories."

The tall man spat carefully into a big brass cuspidor beside the desk. "The best one is that she was asleep and didn't wake up till she heard the shots—and then she turned on the lights an' there he was, on the floor in the doorway. The outer door to the apartment was unlocked—had been unlocked all evening. She says she always left it that way when he was out because he was always losing his key, an' then he could come in without waking her up."

Shane said: "What was she doing in bed at eight-thirty?"

"Bad headache."

Sergeant Gill took a .38 automatic from the drawer of a steel cabinet, handed it to Shane. "No fingerprints," he said—"clean as a whistle."

Shane looked at the gun, put it down on the desk.

The tall man looked at the youth and at Gill, then bobbed his head meaningly towards the door. They both went out. The youth said: "So long, Cap—so long, Mister Shane." Gill closed the door behind him.

Shane was smiling.

The tall man said: "Rigas' wife had these Eastman dicks on his tail—she got anything to do with this?"

"Why?" Shane shrugged. "She wanted a divorce."

"How long they been having trouble?"

"Don't know."

The tall man stood up, stuck his hands in his pockets and went to the window. He spoke over his shoulder: "Didn't you and her used to be pretty good friends?"

Shane didn't answer. His face was entirely expressionless.

The tall man turned and looked at him and then he said: "Well—I guess that's all."

They went out together.

In the corridor Shane made a vague motion with his hand, said: "Be seeing you," went down two flights of stairs and out the door to the street. He stood in the wide arch of the entrance, out of the rain, looked up and down the street for a cab. There was one in front of a drugstore six or seven doors up from the Police Station; he whistled, finally walked swiftly up to it through the blinding rain.

As he got in, the youth in the shiny blue-serge suit came out of the drugstore, scuttled across the sidewalk and climbed in beside him, sat down.

The driver turned around and said: "Where to?"

Shane said: "Wait a minute."

The youth leaned back, put his hand confidentially on Shane's shoulder. He said: "Tell him to drive around the block. I got something to tell you."

The driver looked at Shane, Shane nodded. They swung out from the curb.

The youth said: "I seen Mrs. Rigas about a half a block from the place uptown where Rigas was killed, about ten minutes before we found him."

Shane didn't say anything. He rubbed the side of his face with one hand, glanced at his watch, nodded.

"I was coming back from the delicatessen on the corner, where I got a bite to eat. She was going the same way, on the other side of the street. I wasn't sure it was her at first— I only seen her once when she came in to see Mister Eastman—but there was a car coming down the street and its headlights were pretty bright and I was pretty sure it was her."

Shane said: "Pretty sure."

"Aw hell—it was her." The youth took a soggy cigarette out of his pocket, lighted it.

"Where did she go?"

"That's what I can't figure out. It was raining so damned hard—and the wind was blowing—when I got to our car, that was parked across the street from the Montecito, she'd disappeared." The youth shook his head slowly. "I told my partner about it. He said I was probably wrong, because if it was her she would have called up the office and found out how to spot us, because she would be wanting us to go in with her. He went on down to the corner to get something to eat, an' I sat in the car an' figured that I probably had been wrong, an' then in a few minutes I heard the shots an' the telephone operator come running out."

Shane said: "Did you see Rigas go in?"

The youth shook his head. "No—an' my partner swears he didn't go in while he was on watch. He must've gone in the back way."

Shane took a cigar out of a blue leather case, bit off the end, lighted it. "And you say you were figuring you were wrong about thinking you'd seen her?"

The youth laughed. "Yeah—that's what I figured then. But that ain't what I figure now."

"Why not?"

"Because I pride myself, Mister Shane, on being able to look at a dame what is supposed to have just bumped a guy off, an' knowing whether she did it or not. That's why I'm in the business." He turned his head and looked very seriously at Shane.

Shane smiled faintly in the darkness.

The youth said: "It wasn't McLean." He said it very positively.

Shane said: "Why didn't you tell the Captain about this?"

"Christ! We got to protect our clients."

The cab stopped in front of the drugstore, the driver turned around and looked at Shane questioningly.

Shane blew out a great cloud of gray-blue smoke, glanced at the youth, said: "Where do you want to go?"

"This is oke for me." The youth leaned forward, put his hand on the inside handle of the door. Then he paused, turned his head slightly towards Shane.

"I'm in a spot, Mister Shane. My wife's sick—an' I took

an awful beating on the races the other day, trying to get enough jack for an operation. . . ."

Shane said: "Does anybody besides your partner know about Mrs. Rigas?"

The youth shook his head.

Shane tipped his hat back on his head, drew two fingers across his forehead, said: "I'll see what I can do about it. Where do you live?"

The youth took a card out of his pocket, took out a thin silver pencil and wrote something on it. He handed the card to Shane, said, "So long," and got out of the cab and ran across the sidewalk to the drugstore.

Shane said: "Downtown."

On Twelfth Street, a little way off Sixth Avenue, Shane rapped on the glass, the cab swung to the curb. He told the driver to wait, got out and went down a narrow passageway between two buildings to a green wooden door with a dim electric light above it. He opened the door, knocked on another heavier door set at an angle to the first. It was opened after a little while and he went down four wide steps to a long and narrow room with a bar along one side.

There were seven or eight men at the bar, two white-aproned men behind it: a squat and swarthy Italian and a heavily built Irishman.

Shane went to the far end of the room, leaned on the bar and spoke to the Italian: "What've you got that's best?"

The Italian put a bottle of brandy and a glass on the bar in front of him: Shane took a handkerchief out of his breast pocket, held the glass up to the light, wiped it carefully. He poured a drink, tasted it.

He said: "That's lousy—give me a glass of beer."

The Italian picked up the glass of brandy, drank it, put the bottle away and drew a glass of beer. He skimmed off the foam, put the tall glass on the bar.

He said: "Seventy-five cents."

Shane put a dollar bill on the bar, asked: "Kenny around?"

The Italian shook his head.

Shane said: "Where's the phone?"

The Italian inclined his head towards a narrow door back of Shane. Shane went into the booth and called the

Valmouth, asked for Miss Johnson. When the connection had been made, he said: "Hello, Lorain—what room are you in? . . . All right, stay there until I get back—don't go out for anything—anybody. . . . I'm down at Jack Kenny's. . . . Tell you when I see you. . . . Uh-huh. . . . G'bye. . . ." He hung up and went back to the bar.

The Italian and the Irishman were talking together. The Irishman came down to Shane and said: "Jack's upstairs, asleep. Wha'd you want to see him about?"

"You'd better wake him up—I want to tell him how to keep out of the can." Shane tasted the beer, said: "That's lousy—give me a glass of water."

The Irishman looked at him suspiciously for a minute, put a glass of water on the bar, went to the door at the end of the room. He said: "Who'll I say it is?"

"Shane."

The Irishman disappeared through the door.

He was back in a little while, said: "You can go on up—it's the open door at the top of the stairs."

Shane went back and through the door, across a dark, airless hallway. He lighted a match and found the bottom of the stair, went up. There was a door ajar at the top of the stair through which faint light came, he shoved it open, went in.

Jack Kenny was big and round and bald. He was sitting deep in a worn and battered wicker armchair. He was very drunk.

There was another man, lying face down across the dirty, unmade bed. He was snoring loudly, occasionally exhaled in a long sighing whistle.

Kenny lifted his chin from his chest, lifted bleary eyes to Shane. He said: "Hi, boy?"

Shane asked: "What kind of a rod did you give Del Corey?"

Kenny opened his eyes wide, grinned. He leaned heavily forward, then back, stretched luxuriously.

"I didn't give him any—the louse stole it."

Shane waited.

Kenny was suddenly serious. He said: "What the hell you talking about?"

Shane said: "Charley Rigas was killed tonight with a .38 Smith & Wesson automatic—the safety was knocked off,

27

an' the number on the barrel started with four six six two. . . ."

Kenny stood up suddenly, unsteadily.

Shane said: "I thought you might like to know." He turned and started towards the door.

Kenny said: "Wait a minute."

Shane stopped in the doorway, turned.

All the color had gone out of Kenny's bloated, florid face, leaving it pasty, yellow-white.

He said: "You sure?" He went unsteadily to a little table in the room, picked up an empty bottle, held it up to the light, threw it into a corner.

Shane nodded, said: "Pretty damned dumb for Del to get so steamed up about Lorain an' Charley that he killed Charley—huh? Lorain's been washed up with Charley for months—an' Del ought to've known about it if anybody did. . . ."

Kenny said: "He wasn't worrying about Lorain. It was that little cigarette gal—Thelma, or Selma, or something—that works for Charley. Del's been two-timing Lorain with her for the last couple weeks. That's what he was shooting off his mouth about this afternoon—he had some kind of office on her an' Charley."

Kenny went to a dresser and opened a drawer and took out a bottle of whiskey.

Shane said: "Oh."

He went out and down the dark stair, out to the bar. The glass of beer and the glass of water were on the bar where he had left them. He picked up the glass of water, tasted it, said: "That's lousy," and went out through the front door and the passageway to the cab.

It was a few minutes before eleven when Shane got out of the cab, paid off the driver and went into the Valmouth. The clerk gave him a note that a Mister Arthur had telephoned, would call again in the morning.

Shane went up to his rooms, sat down with his coat and hat on and picked up the telephone.

He said: "Listen, baby—tell the girl that relieves you in the morning that when Mister Arthur calls, I'm out of the city—won't be back for a couple months. He wants to sell me some insurance."

He hung up, looked up the number of 71 in his little black book, called it. A strange voice answered. Shane said: "Is Nick there? . . . Is Pedro there? . . . Never mind—what I want to know is what's Thelma's last name? Thelma, the cigarette girl? . . . Uh-huh. . . . . Never mind who I am— I'm one of your best customers. . . . Uh-huh. . . . How do you spell it? . . . B-u-r-r. . . . You haven't got her telephone number, have you?" . . . The receiver clicked, Shane smiled, hung up.

He found Thelma Burr's address in the telephone directory: a number on West Seventy-Fourth, off Riverside Drive. He got up and went to the table and took several cigars from the humidor, put all but one of them in the blue leather case. He lighted the cigar and stood a little while at one of the windows, staring at the tiny lights in the buildings uptown. Gusts of rain beat against the window and he shuddered suddenly, involuntarily.

He went to a cabinet and took out a square brown bottle, a glass, poured himself a stiff drink. Then he went out, downstairs to the sixteenth floor. He knocked several times at the door of 1611, but there was no answer. He went to the elevator, down to the lobby.

The night clerk said: "That's right, sir—1611, but I think Miss Johnson went out shortly before you came in."

Shane went to the house phone, spoke to the operator: "Did Miss Johnson get any calls after I talked to her around ten-thirty? . . . Right after I called—huh? . . . Thanks."

He went out to a cab, gave the driver the number on Seventy-Fourth Street.

It turned out to be a narrow, five-story apartment house on the north side of the street. Shane told the driver to wait and went up steps, through a heavy door into a dark hall. There were mailboxes on each side of the hall; he lighted a match and started on the left side. The second from the last box on the left bore a name scrawled in pencil that interested him: N. Manos—the apartment number was 414. He went on to the right side of the hall, found the name and the number he was looking for, went up narrow creaking steps to the third floor.

There was no answer at 312.

After a little while, Shane went back downstairs. He

stood in the darkness of the hall for several minutes. Then he went back up to the fourth floor, knocked at 414. There was no answer there either. He tried the door, found it to be locked, went back down to 312.

He stood in the dim light of the hallway a while with his ear close to the door. He heard the outside door downstairs open and close, voices. He went halfway down the stair, waited until the voices had gone away down the corridor on the first floor, went back to the door of 312 and tried several keys in the lock. The sixth key he tried turned almost all the way; he took held of the knob, lifted and pushed, forcing the key at the same time. The lock clicked, gave way, the door swung open.

Shane went into the darkness, closed the door and lighted a match. He found the light switch, pressed it. A floor lamp with a colorful and tasteless batik shade; a smaller table lamp with a black silk handkerchief thrown over it, lighted. The globes were deep amber; the light of the two lamps was barely sufficient to see the brightly papered walls, the mass of furniture in the room. Shane picked his way to the table, jerked the black handkerchief off the table lamp; then there was a little more light.

There was a man on his knees on the floor, against a couch at one end of the little room. The upper part of his body was belly down on the couch and his arms hung limply, ridiculously to the floor; the back of his skull was caved in and the white brightly flowered couch-cover beneath his his head and shoulders was dark red, shiny.

Shane went to him and squatted down and looked at the gashed and bloody side of his face. It was Del Corey.

Shane stood up and crossed the room to an ajar door, pushed it open with his foot. The light over the wash basin was on, covered with several layers of pink silk; the light was very dim.

Thelma Burr was lying on her back on the floor. Her green crepe de chine nightgown was torn, stained. There were black marks on her throat, her breast; her face was puffy, a bruised discolored mask, and her mouth and one cheek were brown-black with iodine. There was a heavy pewter candlestick a little way from one outstretched hand.

Shane knelt, braced his elbow on the edge of the bathtub

and held his ear close to her chest. Her heart was beating faintly.

He stood up swiftly, went out of the bathroom, went to the door. He took out his handkerchief, wiped off the light switch carefully, snapped the lights out. Then he went out and locked the door, wiped the knob, put the key in his pocket and went downstairs, out and across the street to the cab.

The driver jerked his head towards another lone cab halfway down the block. "That hack come up right after we got here," he said. "Nobody got out or nothing. Maybe it's a tail." He stared sharply at Shane.

Shane said: "Probably.". . . He glanced carelessly at the other cab. "You can make yourself a fin if you can get me to the nearest telephone, and then over to 71 East Fifty—in five minutes."

The driver pointed across the street, said: "Garage over there—they ought to have a phone."

Shane ran across to the garage, found a phone and called Central Station, asked for Bill Hayworth. When Hayworth answered, he said: "There's a stiff and a prospective in apartment 312 at———West Seventy-Fourth. Hurry up—the girl's not quite gone. Call you later." He ran out to the waiting cab, climbed in, leaned back and clipped and lighted a cigar, watched the other cab through the rear window. They went over to the Drive, down two blocks, turned east. Shane thought for a while that the other cab wasn't following, but after they'd gone several blocks on Seventy-Second he saw it again. They cut down Broadway to Columbus Circle, across Fifty-Ninth.

In front of 71, Shane jumped out of the cab, said: "That's swell—wait," went swiftly across the sidewalk and pressed the button beneath the red number.

The slit opened, a voice that Shane did not know whispered: "What is it you want?"

Shane said: "In." He stuck his face in the thin shaft of light that came through the slit.

The door was opened and Shane went into the narrow hallway. The man who had let him in was about fifty-five— a slight, thin-faced man with white hair combed straight back from high forehead. He closed the door, bolted it.

Nick was standing behind and a little to one side of the

slight man. He held a blunt blue automatic steadily in his right hand. His chin was on his chest and he stared at Shane narrowly through thick, bushy brows. He jerked his head up suddenly, sharply, said: "Put your hands up, you——!"

Shane smiled slowly, raised his hands slowly as high as his shoulders.

A bell tinkled faintly above the door, the slight white-haired man opened the slit and looked out, closed the slit and opened the door. Another man whom Shane recognized as one of the stud dealers came in. The slight man closed the door.

Nick jerked his head up again, said: "Upstairs." He put the automatic in the pocket of his dinner coat, the muzzle held the cloth out stiff.

Shane turned and went slowly up the stairs, and Nick and the man who followed him in came up behind him. The slight man stayed at the door.

On the second floor, Shane put his hands down as he passed the double-door into the big room, glanced in. There were three people, a man and two women, in earnest and drunken conversation at one of the corner tables. There was a couple at a table against the far wall. With the exception of these and a waiter and the man behind the bar, the room was deserted.

Shane spoke over his shoulder to Nick: "Swell crowd."

Nick took two or three rapid steps, took the automatic out of his pocket and jabbed it against Shane's back, hard. Shane put his hands up again and went up the second flight to the third floor. Nick and the other man followed him. He stopped at the top of the stair, leaned against the balustrade. Nick went past him and knocked at the tall gray door. It was opened in a little while and the three of them went into the room.

Pedro Rigas, Charley's brother, was sitting on one of the big round tables, swinging his feet back and forth. He was very tall and spare and his face was dark, handsome, his features sharply cut.

There was a plump young man with rosy cheeks, bright blue eyes, shingled sand-colored hair, on a straight cane-bottomed chair near Pedro. His legs were crossed and he leaned on one elbow on the table. There was a heavy nickeled revolver on the table near his elbow. He stared at Shane with interest.

Lorain Rigas was sitting on a worn imitation-leather couch against one wall. She was leaning forward with her elbows on her knees, her hands over her eyes. She had taken off the small suede hat, her dull black hair curved in damp arabesques over her white forehead and throat and hands.

The little Eastman operative was half sitting, half lying on the floor against the wall near the couch. His face was a pulpy mass of bruised, beaten flesh; one arm was up, half covering the lower part of his face, the other was propped in the angle of the floor and wall. He was sobbing quietly, his body shook.

Pedro Rigas looked at the dealer who had come in with Shane and Nick, nodded towards Shane, asked: "You bring him in?"

Nick said: "He came in—by himself." He grinned mirthlessly at Shane.

Shane was staring sleepily at Lorain Rigas.

She lifted her face, looked at him helplessly. "Somebody called up a little while after I talked to you," she said—"said it was the night clerk—said you were waiting for me out in front of the hotel. I went down and they smacked me into a cab, brought me over here."

Shane nodded slightly.

She turned her eyes towards the Eastman man on the floor. "He was here," she went on, "an' they were beating hell out of him. I don't know where they picked him up."

Shane said: "Probably at the Station, after he talked to me. They've been tailing me all night—since I left the hotel to go over an' talk to the captain. That's how they knew you were at the hotel—they saw you come in around nine— an' they got the fake Johnson name from the register."

Pedro Rigas was smiling coldly at Shane, swinging his feet back and forth nervously.

He said: "One of you two,"—he jerked his head towards the girl—"killed Charley. I find out pretty soon which one— or by God I kill you both."

Shane had put his hands down. He held them in front of

him and looked down at them, stroked the back of one with the palm of the other. Then he looked up at the rosy-cheeked young man, questioned Rigas: "Executioner?" He smiled slightly, sarcastically.

Lorain Rigas stood up suddenly, faced Pedro. She said: "You fool! Can't you get it through that nut of yours that Del killed Charley? Dear God!"—she made a hopeless gesture. "Read the papers—the gun they found was the one Del swiped from Jack Kenny this afternoon. Jack'll verify that."

Pedro's face was cold and hard and expressionless when he looked at her. "What were you doing up there?"

"I told you!" she almost screamed. "I went to warn Charley that Del was after him! I heard the shots when I was halfway upstairs—got out."

Shane was looking at Lorain Rigas and there was a dim mocking glitter in his eyes.

She glanced at him, said: "I didn't tell you about that, Dick, because I was afraid you'd get ideas. You wouldn't trust your own mother across the street, you know."

Shane nodded gently, slowly.

He turned to Pedro. "Where do *I* come in?" he said. "I went from here to the hotel—an' I was there till about a quarter of ten. . . ."

The dealer, who was still standing near the door, spoke for the first time: "No. After you left here, you didn't get to the hotel till about ten minutes of nine. I found that out from a friend of mine—a bellhop."

Lorain Rigas looked from the dealer to Shane. Her eyes were wide, surprised. She said: "My God!"

Pedro stopped swinging his feet suddenly. He said: "Where did you go after you left here?" He was staring at Shane and his eyes were thin heavily fringed slits.

Shane was silent a moment. Then he reached slowly, deliberately towards his inside pocket, smiled at Lorain Rigas, said: "May I smoke?"

Pedro stood up suddenly.

The rosy-cheeked youth stood up, too. The revolver glistened in his hand and he went swiftly to Shane, patted his pockets, his hips, felt under his arms. He finished, stepped back a pace.

Shane took out the blue case, took out a cigar and lighted it.

It was silent except for the choked sobbing of the little Eastman man.

Nick came suddenly forward, took Shane by the shoulder, shook him. Nick said: "You answer Pedro when he asks you a question."

Shane turned slowly and frowned at Nick. He looked down at Nick's hand on his shoulder, said slowly: "Take your hand off me, you——!" He looked back at Pedro. "Ask Nick where he went tonight."

Pedro jerked his head impatiently.

Shane took the cigar out of his mouth, said: "Did you know that Thelma—downstairs—is Nick's gal?" He hesitated a moment, glanced swiftly at Nick. "An' did you know that Charley's been playing around with her?"

Pedro was staring at Nick. His mouth was a little open.

Shane went on: "Nick knew it. . . ."

He whirled suddenly and smashed his left fist down hard on Nick's broad forearm, grabbed for the automatic with his right hand. The automatic fell, clattered on the floor. Shane and Nick and the rosy-cheeked young man all dived for it, but the young man was a little faster; he stood up grinning widely, murderously—a gun in each hand.

Pedro said: "Go on."

Shane didn't say anything. He was looking at Nick and his eyes were bright, interested—he was smiling a little.

Pedro snapped at the dealer: "Go downstairs an' send Mario up—you stay at the door."

The dealer went out and closed the door.

They were all very quiet. Nick was staring at the automatic in the young man's hand and there was a very silly, far-away expression on his face. Shane was watching Nick like a vivisectionist about to make the crucial incision. Lorain Rigas was sitting down again on the couch with her hands over her eyes.

Pedro only waited, looked at the floor.

The door opened and the slight, white-haired man came in. Pedro said: "What time did Nick go out tonight?"

The slight man looked at Nick bewilderedly. He cleared his throat, said: "Nick went out right after Charley went home. He said there wasn't any business anyway, an' he wanted to go to a picture-show, an' would I take the door for a while. He came back some time around nine. . . ."

Pedro said: "All right—go on back downstairs."

The slight man gestured with one hand. "You seen me on the door when you went out right after we heard about Charley," he said. "Wasn't it all right for me to be on the door?"

"Sure." Pedro was looking at Nick. "Sure—only I thought Nick was down in the basement or something—I didn't know he'd gone out."

The slight man shrugged and went out and closed the door.

Shane said evenly: "Nick had a hunch that Charley was going to Thelma's. He didn't follow Charley, but he jumped in a cab, probably, an went to her place. He didn't find Charley—but he found Del Corey."

Lorain Rigas put her hands down and looked up at Shane. Her face was drawn, white.

"That's what Del went there for," Shane went on— "expecting to find Charley. Del's been making a big play for Thelma—an' he knew about Charley and her—was cock-eyed an' burnt up an' aimed to rub Charley." Shane was watching Nick narrowly. "Thelma must've calmed Del down—Nick found them there. . . ." Shane turned his eyes towards Lorain Rigas. ". . . And caved in Del's head."

Lorain Rigas stood up, screamed.

Pedro crossed to her swiftly, put one hand over her mouth, the other on her back, pushed her back down on the couch gently.

Shane said: "Then Nick beat the hell out of Thelma, made her admit that Charley had been in the woodpile, too, damn' near killed her."

He was looking at Nick again.

"He dragged what was left of her into the bathroom and poured some iodine on her mouth, an' put the candlestick that he'd smacked Del with in her hands so it would look like she'd killed Del an' then committed suicide."

Nick turned to stare at Shane vacantly.

Shane was puffing out great clouds of blue-gray smoke, seemed to be enjoying himself hugely.

"She wasn't quite dead, though," he went on. He

glanced at his watch. "The law ought to be over there by now—getting her testimony."

Pedro said: "Hurry up."

Shane shrugged. "Nick took the gun that Del got from Jack Kenny, jumped up to Charley's. He knew he was in a good spot to let Charley have it because Charley and I had that argument tonight—an' it'd look like me—or he could make it look like me. Charley evidently stopped some place on the way home—Nick got there first and either stuck Charley up in the corridor and took him into the apartment to kill him, or sneaked in—the door was unlocked—and waited in the dark. Then he went out the back way—the way Charley came in—and came back down here."

Pedro went to the door, turned to Shane, said: "You and the lady go."

Shane gestured towards the Eastman man. "What about him?"

"We'll fix him up—give him some money. It is too bad." Pedro smiled, opened the door.

Shane looked at Nick. Nick's face was pasty, yellow, still wore the silly, far-away expression.

Lorain Rigas stood up and took up her hat and went to Shane.

They went together to the door, out into the hallway. Pedro leaned over the balustrade, called down to the little man at the outside door: "Okay."

Shane and the girl went downstairs, past the doors of the dark and empty barroom, down to the street floor.

The slight, white-haired man and the dealer were whispering together. The slight man opened the door for them, said: "Good night—come again."

They went out and got into the cab.

Shane said: "Valmouth."

It had stopped raining for the moment, but the streets were still black and glistening and slippery.

He tossed the cigar out through the narrow space of open window, leaned back, said: "Am I a swell dick?—or am I a swell dick?"

Lorain Rigas didn't answer. Her elbow was on the arm

37

rest, her chin in her hand. She stared out the window blankly.

"You're not very appreciative." Shane smiled to himself, was silent a little while.

The light held them up at Fifth Avenue. Theater traffic was heavy in spite of the weather.

Shane said: "The only thing I'm not quite sure about is whether you went to Charley's to warn him—or whether you'd heard about Del and Thelma—thought that the day Del was yelping about shooting Charley, in front of witnesses, was a swell time for you to shoot Charley yourself."

She did not answer.

As the cab curved into Sixth Avenue, she said: "Where did you go after you left 71—before you went back to the hotel?"

Shane laughed. "That lousy alibi held up with the captain," he said. "He didn't question it." He unbuttoned the top button of his topcoat, took something wrapped in tissue paper out of his inside pocket. "You know what a sucker I am for auction sales?"

She nodded.

He unfolded the tissue paper and took out a platinum-mounted diamond ring. The stone was large, pure white, very beautiful.

He said: "Pip?"

She nodded again.

He put the ring back in the tissue paper, folded it, put it back in his pocket.

The cab slid to the curb in front of the Valmouth.

Shane said: "Where you going?"

She shook her head.

He said: "You keep the cab." He pressed a bill into her hand, said: "This'll take care of it—why don't you take a nice long ride?"

He brushed her forehead lightly with his lips and got out of the cab and went into the hotel.

I knocked on the door at the end of the hall. It was cold in the hall, almost dark. I knocked again, and Bella's voice said: "Come in," faintly; then she said: "Oh—it's locked." The key scratched in the lock and the door opened and I went into the room.

It was very hot in there. It was dark, with only a little light from a gas heater. There was a little more light that came through a short corridor from the kitchen, but it was pretty dark.

Bella closed the door and went over to the davenport and sat down. She was near the heater, and the yellow light flickered over the lower part of her face.

I took off my coat and put it on a chair. Bella kept scraping her teeth lightly over her lower lip. Her teeth were like a little animal's and she ran them over her soft lower lip rapidly, like an animal. The light from the heater was bright on the lower part of her face.

I went through the short corridor to the kitchen. The bathroom door was open; I glanced in as I passed and Gus Schaeffer turned his head and looked over his shoulder at me. He was standing at the basin with his back to the door and when he turned his head to look at me his face was awful. His skin was damp and gray and his eyes had something leaden and dying in them.

I said: "Hi, Gus," and went in to the kitchen.

There was a man sitting on one of the benches at one side of the narrow breakfast table. The table was set lengthwise into a niche, with a bench at each side, and the man on one of the benches was sitting with his back in the corner of the niche, his knees drawn up, his feet on the outside end of the bench. His head was back against the wall and his eyes and mouth were open. There was a thin knife handle sticking out of one side of his throat.

Gus came out of the bathroom and stood behind me in the doorway.

There were several nearly empty glasses on the table. One had fallen to the floor, broken into many glittering pieces.

I looked at the glass and I looked up at the man again. I think I said: "——" very softly.

"I did it. I did it and I didn't know it. I was blind. . . ." Gus was clawing at my arm.

Bella came through the corridor and stood behind him. She looked very scared, very beautiful.

She said huskily: "Gus was terribly drunk. Frank said something out of turn and Gus picked up the knife and stuck it into his neck. He choked—I guess—"

She looked at the dead man, and then her eyes turned up white in their sockets and she fainted.

Gus turned around and almost fell down trying to catch her. He said: "Oh, baby—baby!" He took her up in his arms and carried her back into the living-room.

I followed him in and switched on the lights. He put Bella on the davenport. I watched him bend over her and flick ice water across her face with his fingers, from a pitcher; he rubbed her hands and wrists, and tried to force a little whiskey between her clenched pale lips. He kept saying: "Oh, baby—baby," over and over. I sat down.

He sat on the edge of the davenport and looked at me while he rubbed and patted Bella's hands.

"You better telephone," he said. Then he looked at Bella a long time. "I did it—see—I did it; only I didn't know about it. I was cockeyed—"

I nodded. I said: "Sure, Gus," and I leaned forward and picked up the telephone.

Gus was looking at Bella's white beautiful face. He bobbed his head up and down mechanically.

I said: "What's the best play—self-defense?"

He turned suddenly. "I don't care—no play at all." He dropped her hand and stood up. "Only I did it myself. She didn't have anything to do with it. She was in here. . . ." He came towards me, shaking his finger at me, speaking very earnestly.

I said: "Maybe I can get Neilan. The longer we let it go, the worse it'll be."

I dialed a number.

Neilan was a short chubby man with a strangely long face, a high bony forehead. He and Frank had been partners in a string of distilleries for almost five years. He said: "When did *you* get here, Red?"

"Bella called me up and told me something had happened—I live around the corner."

I was sitting near the door that led in to the kitchen. Bella was sitting in the middle of the davenport, leaning forward with her elbows on her knees, staring vacantly into the brightness of the heater. Gus was sitting in a straight-backed chair in the middle of the room.

Neilan had been walking around looking at the pictures on the walls. He sat down straddling an arm of the davenport.

"So you were so drunk you don't remember?" Neilan was looking at Gus.

Gus nodded. Bella looked up at him for a moment and nodded a little and then looked back into the fire.

There was a light tap at the door and it opened and a big man came in quietly and closed the door behind him. He wore glasses and his soft black hat was tilted over the back of his head. I think his name was McNulty, or McNutt—something like that. He said: "Ed's downstairs with a couple of the boys."

"They can wait downstairs." Neilan turned his head a little and looked at Bella out of the corners of his eyes. "So Gus was so drunk he don't remember?"

Gus stood up. He said: "——damn it! Pat—I was so drunk I didn't know any better, but I wasn't so drunk I don't know it was me. Lay off Bella—she was in here. . . ."

"She didn't say so."

Bella said: "I was nearly asleep and I could hear Gus and Frank talking in the kitchen and then they didn't talk any more. After a while I got up and went out in the kitchen—Frank was like he is now, and Gus was out—with his head on the table."

Her chin was in her hands, and her head bobbed up and

down when she talked. Gus was sitting down again, on the edge of the chair.

Neilan grinned at McNulty. He said: "What do you think, Mac?"

McNulty went over to Bella and reached down and put one big finger under her chin and jerked her head back.

"I think she's a liar," he said.

Gus stood up.

McNulty turned as if that had been what he wanted. He hit Gus very hard in the face, twice. Gus fell down and rolled over on his side. He pulled his knees up and moaned a little.

McNulty took off his coat and folded it carefully and put it on a chair. He went to Gus and kicked him hard in the chest and then kicked his head several times. Gus tried to protect himself with his arms. He didn't make any more noise but put his arms up and tried to protect himself. He tried to get up once and McNulty kicked him in the stomach and he fell down and lay quietly. In a little while, McNulty stopped kicking him and sat down. He was panting. He took off his hat and took a handkerchief out of his pocket and wiped his face.

I looked at Neilan. "I called you," I said, "because I thought you'd give Gus a break. . . ."

He said: "You ought to of called the police. They'd be after giving Gus a break, and your lady friend here"—he jerked his head at Bella—"with a length of hose."

Bella was leaning back on the davenport with her hands up to her face. She stared at Gus and tried to look at McNulty.

McNulty smiled, said: "Sure—why don't you call a cop? Frankie had everybody from the Chief down on his payroll—they'll have to go back to working for the city." He was out of breath, spoke unevenly.

Bella stood up and started to go towards the door, and Neilan stood up too, and put one hand over her mouth and one on her back. He held her like that for a minute and then he pushed her back down on the davenport.

McNulty got up then and stooped over and took hold of the back of Gus' shirt collar and pulled him up a little way.

McNulty said: "Come on, boy—we'll get some air."

Gus' shirt collar started to tear and McNulty cupped his other hand around the back of Gus' neck and jerked him up on his feet. Gus couldn't stand by himself; McNulty stood there holding him with his arm around his shoulders. Gus' face was in pretty bad shape.

McNulty said: "Come on, boy," again and started guiding Gus towards the door.

Neilan said: "Wait a minute, Mac."

McNulty turned and stared vacantly at Neilan for a minute and then pushed Gus down in a big chair. He sat down on the arm of the chair and took out his handkerchief and wiped Gus' face.

Neilan went out into the kitchen. He was out there two or three minutes without making any noise, then he snapped off the light and came back. He turned off the lights in the living room too, and it was dark except for the faint yellow light from the heater.

Neilan went back and sat down at the end of the davenport, out of the light. The light rippled over Bella's face, and after a while, when my eyes were used to the darkness, I could make out dark shapes where McNulty and Gus sat—and Neilan.

It was so dark and quiet except for the sharp sound of Gus' breathing. There wasn't anything to look at except Bella and she was leaning back with her eyes closed and her face very still.

It got on my nerves after several minutes and I said: "What's it all about, Pat?"

Neilan didn't answer, so I leaned forward in my chair, but I didn't get up. I sat there with all my muscles tight.

Then I heard something moving out in the kitchen. I don't know whether anybody else heard it, but I know there was a sound out there like something moving across the floor.

I stood up and I couldn't speak. I didn't hear the sound again but I stood there without moving, and then Bella started talking. She talked in a conversational tone, with her head back, her eyes closed:

"Frank came here to see me. He's been coming to see me every night for four nights. He brought along a lot of lousy whiskey and got Gus drunk, and he got drunk too. He got Gus drunk once before and tried to sell me an idea. He wouldn't give up."

43

She stopped talking a moment and the light beat up and down on her face. She was very beautiful then.

"He made a crack tonight while Gus was in the bathroom about telling Gus about Red and me. . . ."

She opened her eyes and looked towards me in the darkness a minute, and then closed her eyes and went on:

"I was scared. I called Red while they were raising hell in the kitchen and he came over and I let him in. We listened to them for a few minutes from in here in the dark, and then when Frank got to talking about what a great guy Red was, and started getting dirty about it, Red went in there very quickly and killed him. I guess Gus was too far gone to see it or know anything about it."

She stopped talking again and it was quiet.

"Then Red beat it and I stayed in here a while and then I went out like I told you and woke up Gus. He thought I did it, I guess. I called Red again. . . ."

Neilan got up and went over and switched on the lights.

McNulty got up too and stood there blinking, staring stupidly at Bella.

I went over and got my hat and coat and put them on. I stood looking at Bella for a while after I had put on my coat. She was still leaning back with her eyes closed. She was one of the most beautiful women I have ever seen.

Neilan opened the door and McNulty and I went out into the hall. It was very cold there after the intense heat of the room. Then Neilan closed the door and the three of us went downstairs.

There was a small touring car at the curb, with the side-curtains on. There were two men whom I had never seen before in the front seat, and another man standing on the sidewalk. The engine was running.

McNulty opened the door and got in the back seat, and then I got in, and then Neilan. There wasn't anything else to do. I sat between them, and Neilan said: "Let's go."

We went down the street slowly. The man who had been standing on the sidewalk didn't get into the car; he stood there looking after us. I turned around a little and looked at him through the rear window; as we turned the corner, he went on back up the street, the other way.

When we got out of town a ways we went faster. It was very cold.

I said: "Hurry up."

Neilan turned and grinned at me. I could see his face a little as we passed a street light. He said: "Hurry up—what?"

"Hurry up." The cold was beginning to get in to the pit of my stomach, and my legs. I wanted to be able to stand up. I wanted it standing up, if I could.

Neilan glanced out the rear window. He said: "I think our tail light's out."

The car slowed, stopped. We were pretty well out in the country by that time and the road was dark.

Neilan said: "See if we've got a tail light, Mac."

McNulty grunted and reached up and opened the door and heaved himself up into the door. He stooped and put one foot out on the running board, and then Neilan reached in front of me very quickly. There was a gun in his hand and he put it close to McNulty's back and shot him three times. The explosions were very close together. McNulty's knees crumpled up and he fell out of the car on his face.

The car started again and the man who sat next to the driver reached back and slammed the door shut hard.

Neilan cleared his throat. He said: "Frank's number has been up a long time. He's been tipping our big deliveries, South; we haven't got a truck through for two months."

I could feel the blood getting back into my arms and legs. I wasn't so cold and I could breathe without pain.

"McNulty was in it with him. McNulty was in the outfit downstate. We found out about that last night."

We rode on for a little while and nobody said anything.

"If the dame sticks to her beef," Neilan went on, "the scarcer you are, the better. If she doesn't, Gus'll stand it. You can't do yourself any good around here any more anyway."

Pretty soon we stopped at a little interurban station where I could get a car in to the city.

I had to wait a while. I sat in the station where it was warm, and thought about Bella. After a while the car came.

45

ONE, TWO, THREE

I'd been in Los Angeles waiting for this Healey to show for nearly a week. According to my steer, he'd taken a railroad company in Quebec for somewhere in the neighborhood of a hundred and fifty grand on a swarm of juggled options or something. That's a nice neighborhood.

My information said further that he was headed west and that he dearly loved to play cards. I do, too.

I'll take three off the top, please.

I missed him by about two hours in Chicago and spent the day going around to all the ticket offices, getting chummy with agents, finally found out Healey had bought a ticket to L A, so I fanned on out there and cooled.

Pass.

Sunday afternoon I ran into an op for Eastern Investigators, Inc., named Gard, in the lobby of the Roosevelt. We had a couple drinks and talked about this and that. He was on the Coast looking for a gent named Healey. He was cagey about who the client was, but Eastern handles mostly missing persons, divorces, stuff like that.

Monday morning Gard called me and said the Salt Lake branch of his outfit had located Healey in Caliente, Nevada. He said he thought I might like to know. I told him I wasn't interested and thanked him and then I rented a car in a U Drive place and drove up to Caliente.

I got there about four in the afternoon and spotted Healey in the second joint I went into. He was sitting in a stud game with five of the home boys and if they were a fair sample of local talent I figured I had plenty of time.

Healey was a big man with a round cheery face, smooth pink skin. His mouth was loose and wet and his eyes were light blue. I think his eyes were the smallest I've ever seen. They were set very wide apart.

He won and lost pretty evenly, but the game wasn't worth

47

a nickel. The home boys were old-timers and played close to their vests and Healey's luck was the only thing that kept him even. He finally scared two of them out of a seventy- or eighty-dollar pot and that made him feel so good that he got up and came over to the bar and ordered drinks for the boys at the table. He ordered lemonade for himself.

I said: "Excuse me, but haven't I seen you around Lonnie Thompson's in Detroit?" Lonnie makes a book and I had most of my dope on Healey from him.

He smiled and said: "Maybe," and asked me what I drank.

I ordered whiskey.

He asked me if I'd been in town long and I said I'd just driven up from L A to look things over and that things didn't look so hot and that I would probably drive back to L A that night or the next morning.

I bought him another lemonade and had another whiskey and we talked about Detroit. In a little while he went back to the table and sat down.

That was enough for a beginning. I had registered myself with him as one of the boys. I went out and drove a couple of blocks to the Pine Hotel and took a room. The Pine was practically the only hotel in town, but I flipped the register back a day or so and found Healey's name to make sure. Then I went up and washed and lay down to smoke a cigarette and figure out the details.

According to Lonnie Thompson, Healey was a cash boy—carried his dough in paper and traveler's cheques. I couldn't be sure of that but it was enough. The point was to get him to L A and in to one or two or three places where I could work on him.

I guess I must have slept almost an hour because it was dark when I woke up. Somebody was knocking at the door and I got up and stumbled over and switched on the light and opened the door. I was too sleepy to take Healey big—I mumbled something about coming in and sitting down, and I went over to the basin and put some cold water on my face.

When I turned around he was sitting on the bed looking scared. I offered him a cigarette and he took it and his hand was shaking.

He said: "Sorry I woke you up like that."

I said: "That's all right," and then he leaned forward and spoke in a very low voice:

"I've got to get out of here right away. I want to know how much it's worth to you to take me down to Los Angeles."

I almost fell off the chair. My first impulse was to yell, "Sure," and drag him down to the car; but he was scared of something and when a man's scared is a swell time to find out what it's all about.

I stalled. I said: "Oh, that's all right," sort of hesitantly.

He said: "Listen. . . . I got here Saturday morning. I was going to stay here long enough to establish residence and then apply for one of those quick divorces, under the Nevada law.

"My wife has been on my tail six weeks with a blackmail gag," he went on. "She's here. When I got back to the hotel a little while ago she came into my room and put on an act."

I thought then I knew who Gard's client was.

"She came in this afternoon. She's got the room next to mine."

He was silent so long that I laughed a little and said: "So what?" ·

"I've got to duck, quick," he went on. "She's a bad actor. She came into my room and put on an act. She's got a guy with her that's supposed to be her brother and he's a bad actor, too. You said you were going to drive back to L A. I saw your name on the register when I came in and I thought you might take me along. I can't rent a car here and there isn't a train till midnight."

He pulled the biggest roll I ever saw out of his pocket and skimmed off a couple notes. "If it's a question of money. . . ."

I shook my head with what I hoped was a suggestion of dignity. I said: "I'd decided to go back myself tonight. It will be a pleasure to take you, Mister Healey," and I got up and put on my coat. "How about your stuff?"

He looked blank until I said: "Luggage," and then he said: "That's all right—I'll leave it." He smiled again. "I travel light."

At the top of the stairs he whispered: "This is sure a big lift." Then he remembered that he had to sneak up to his

49

room to get something and said he'd meet me at the car. I told him where it was. He said he'd paid his hotel bill.

I went on downstairs and checked out.

My car was wedged in between a Ford truck and a light-blue Chrysler roadster. There was plenty of room ahead of the roadster, so I went up and snapped off the hand-brake and pushed it ahead about eight feet. Then I got into my car and leaned back and waited.

The whole layout looked pretty bad, what with him scared to death of a deal he admitted was blackmail and all. He said he didn't want his luggage and then, right on top of it, he had to go up to his room to get something. That would be taking a chance on running into the wife again. I wondered if she was his wife.

I couldn't figure out how a wife could blackmail a husband while she was jumping from state to state with a man who was "supposed" to be her brother; but then almost anything is possible in Nevada.

After about five minutes I began to get nervous. I opened the door of the car and stepped out on the sidewalk, and as I closed the door there were five shots close together some place upstairs in the hotel.

I can take trouble or leave it alone; only I always take it. Like a sap, I went into the hotel.

The clerk was a big blond kid with glasses. He came out from behind the counter as I went in the door; we went upstairs together, two or three at a time.

There was a man in long woolly underwear standing in the corridor on the third floor and he pointed to a door and we went in. Healey was lying flat on his face in the middle of the room, and beyond him, close to the wall, was the body of a woman, also face downward.

The clerk turned a beautiful shade of green; he stood there staring at Healey. I went over and rolled the woman over on her back. She couldn't have been much over twenty-two or three; little, gray-eyed, blonde. There was a knife in her side, under the arm. There was a .38 automatic near her outstretched hand. She was very dead.

The man in the woolly underwear peeked in and then hurried across the hall and into another room. I could hear him yelling the news to somebody there.

50

I went over and tapped the clerk on the shoulder and pointed at the girl. The clerk swallowed a couple of times, said: "Miss Mackay," and looked back at Healey. He was hypnotized by the way Healey's back looked. Hamburger.

Then about two dozen people came into the room all at once.

The sheriff had been in the pool-hall across the street. He rolled Healey over and said: "This is Mister Healey," as if he'd made a great discovery.

I said: "Uh-huh. He's been shot."

I guess the sheriff didn't like the way I said it very well. He glanced at the clerk and then asked me who I was. I told him my name and the clerk nodded and the sheriff scratched his head and went over and looked at the girl. I wanted to say that she'd been knifed, but I restrained myself.

Shaggy underwear was back with his pants on. He said he hadn't heard anything except somebody swearing and then, suddenly, the shots.

I asked him how long after the shots it had been when he came into the corridor and he said he wasn't sure, but it was somewhere around half a minute.

The first interesting thing that turned up was that it wasn't Healey's room—it was Miss Mackay's room. His was next door. That probably meant that Healey had deliberately gone into her room; that she hadn't surprised him in his room while he was getting something he'd forgotten.

Number two was that the knife was Healey's. Half a dozen people had seen him with it. It was an oversize jack-knife with a seven-inch blade—one of the kind that snaps open when you press a spring. Somebody said Healey had a habit of playing mumbletypeg with it when he was trying to outsit a raise or scare somebody into splitting a pot.

Number three was the topper. The dough was gone. The sheriff and a couple of deputies searched Healey and went through both rooms with a fine-tooth comb. They weren't looking for big money because they didn't know about it; they were looking for evidence.

All they found on Healey were four hundred-dollar bills tucked into his watch pocket, and the usual keys, cigarettes, whatnot. There were no letters or papers of any kind. There was one big suitcase in his room and it was full of dirty clothes. The roll he'd flashed on me was gone.

In the next half-hour I found out a lot of things. The girl had come to the hotel alone. No one else had checked in that day, except myself. The door to the girl's room was about twenty feet from the top of the back stairs and there was a side-door to the hotel that they didn't lock until ten o'clock.

It looked like a cinch for the man Healey had told me about, the one who was supposed to be Miss Mackay's brother.

Healey had probably gone upstairs to take care of the girl. I knew that his being scared of her was on the level because I know bona-fide fear when I see it. She evidently had plenty on him. He'd arranged his getaway with me and then gone up to carve the girl, shut her up forever.

The alleged brother had come in the side-door and had walked in on the knife act and opened up Healey's back with the automatic at about six feet.

Then he'd grabbed the roll and whatever else Healey had in his pocket that was of any value—maybe a book of traveler's cheques—had tossed the gun on the floor and screwed back down the back stairway and out the side-door. Something like that. It wasn't entirely plausible, but it was all I could figure right then.

By the time I'd figured that much out the sheriff had it all settled that Healey had knifed the girl and then she'd plugged him five times, in a ten-inch square in his back. With about three inches of steel in her heart.

That was what the sheriff said so I let it go. They didn't know about the brother and I didn't want to complicate their case for them. And I did want a chance to look for that roll without interference.

When I got out to the car the blue Chrysler was gone. That wasn't important except that I wondered who had been going away from the hotel when it looked like everybody in town was there or on the way there.

I didn't get much information at the station. The agent said he'd just come on duty; the telegraph operator had been there all afternoon but he was out to supper. I found him in a lunch-room across the street and he said there'd been a half-dozen or so people get off the afternoon train from Salt Lake; but the girl had been alone and he wasn't sure who the other people had been except three of four hometowners. That was no good.

I tried to find somebody else who had been in the station when the train came in but didn't have any luck. They couldn't remember.

I went back to the car and that made me think about the blue Chrysler again. It was just possible that the Mackay girl had come down from Salt Lake by rail, and the boy-friend or brother or whatever he was had driven down. It didn't look particularly sensible but it was an idea. Maybe they didn't want to appear to be traveling together or something.

I stopped at all the garages and gas-stations I could find but I couldn't get a line on the Chrysler. I went back to the hotel and looked at the register and found out that Miss Mackay had put down Chicago as her home, and I finagled around for a half hour and talked to the sheriff and the clerk and everybody who looked like they wanted to talk but I didn't get any more angles.

The sheriff said he'd wired Chicago because it looked like Healey and Miss Mackay were both from Chicago, and that he'd found a letter in one of Healey's old coats from a Chicago attorney. The letter was about a divorce, and the sheriff had a hunch that Miss Mackay was Mrs Healey.

I had a sandwich and a piece of pie in the hotel restaurant and bundled up and went out and got in the car and started for L A.

I didn't get up till around eleven o'clock Tuesday morning. I had breakfast in my room and wired a connection in Chi to send me all he could get on Miss Mackay and her brother. I called the desk and got the number of Gard's room and on the way down stopped in to see him.

He was sitting in his nightshirt by the window, reading the morning papers. I sat down and asked him how he was enjoying his vacation and he said swell, and then he said: "I see by the papers that our friend Healey had an accident."

I nodded.

Gard chuckled: "Tch, tch, tch. His wife will sure be cut up."

53

I smiled a little and said, "Uh-huh," and Gard looked up and said: "What the hell are you grinning about and what do you mean: Uh-huh?"

I told him that according to my paper Mrs Healey was the lady who had rubbed Healey—the lady who was on her way back East in a box.

Gard shook his head intelligently and said: "Wrong. That one was an extra. Mrs Healey is alive and kicking and one of the sweetest dishes God ever made."

I could see that he was going to get romantic so I waited and he told me that Mrs Healey had been the agency's client in the East and that she'd come in from Chicago Monday morning by plane and that he'd met her in the agency office, and then he went on for five or ten minutes about the color of her eyes and the way she wore her hair, and everything.

Gard was pretty much of a ladies' man. He told it with gestures.

Along with the poetry he worked in the information that Mrs Healey, as he figured it, had had some trouble with Healey and that they'd split up and that she wanted to straighten it all out. That was the reason she'd wired the Salt Lake office of his agency to locate Healey. And almost as soon as they'd found Healey he'd shoved off for L A and the agency had wired her in Chicago to that effect. She'd arrived the morning Healey had been spotted in Caliente and had decided to wait in L A for him.

Gard said he had helped her find an apartment. He supposed the agency had called her up and told her the bad news about Healey. He acted like he was thinking a little while and then asked me if I didn't think he ought to go over and see if he could help her in any way. "Comfort her in her bereavement," was the way he put it.

I said: "Sure—we'll both go."

Gard didn't go for that very big, but I told him that my having been such a pal of Healey's made it all right.

We went.

Mrs Healey turned out a great deal better than I had expected from Gard's glowing description. As a matter of fact she was swell. She was very dark, with dark blue eyes and blue-black hair; her clothes were very well done and her voice was cultivated, deep. When she acknowledged Gard's half-stammered introduction, inclined her head towards me and asked us to sit down, I saw that she had been crying.

Gard had done pretty well in the way of helping her find an apartment. It was a big luxurious duplex in the Garden Court on Kenmore.

She smiled at Gard. "It's very nice of you gentlemen to call," she said.

I said we wanted her to know how sorry we were about it all and that I had known Healey in Detroit, and if there was anything we could do—that sort of thing.

There wasn't much else to say. There wasn't much else said.

She asked Gard to forgive her for bothering him so much the previous evening with her calls, but that she'd been nervous and worried and kept thinking that maybe Healey had arrived in L A after the agency was closed and that she hadn't been notified. They'd been watching the trains of course.

Gard said that was all right and got red and stammered some more. He was stunned by the lady. So was I. She was a pip.

She said she thought she'd stay in California and she told us delicately that she'd made arrangements for Healey's body to be shipped to his folks in Detroit.

Finally I said we'd better go and Gard nodded and we got up. She thanked us again for coming and a maid helped us with our coats and we left.

Gard said he had to go downtown so I took a cab and went back to the hotel. There was a wire from Chicago: JEWEL MACKAY TWO CONVICTIONS EXTORTION STOP WORKS WITH HUSBAND ARTHUR RAINES ALIAS J L MAXWELL STOP LEFT CHICAGO WEDNESDAY FOR LOS ANGELES WITH RAINES STOP DESCRIPTION MACKAY FOUR ELEVEN ONE HUNDRED TWO BLONDE GRAY EYES RAINES FIVE SIX ONE HUNDRED TWENTY-FIVE RED BROWN EYES STOP MAY LOCATE THROUGH BROTHER WILLIAM RAINES REAL ESTATE SOUTH LABREA REGARDS

ED.

I got the number of Raines' real estate office from the telephone book and took a cab and went down and looked it

55

over. I didn't go in. Then I told the driver to take me to the Selwyn Apartments on Beverly Boulevard. That was the place the telephone book had listed as Raines' residence.

It took a half-hour of jabbering about spark plugs with the Bohunk in the Selwyn garage to find out that Mister Raines had gone out about ten o'clock with another gentleman, and what Mister Raines looked like and what kind of a car he drove. The gentleman who had been with him was tall— or maybe he was short. Or maybe it had been a lady. The Bohunk wasn't sure.

I jockeyed the cab around to a good spot in the cross street and went into the drug-store on the opposite corner and drank Coca-Colas. Along about the fifth Coca-Cola the car I was looking for pulled up in front of the Selwyn. A medium-sized middle-aged man who I figured to be the brother got out of the driver's seat and went into the apartment house. The other man in the car moved over into the driver's seat and started west on Beverly. By that time I was back in the cab and after him.

Of course I couldn't be sure it was Raines. It looked like a little man. I had to take that chance.

We followed the car out Beverly to Western, up Western. I wondered what had become of the blue Chrysler. Then we drew up close behind Raines' car at an intersection and I nearly fell out the window. The man in the car ahead turned around and looked back; we looked smack at one another for five seconds.

I'd seen him before! I'd seen him the night before in Miss Mackay's room at the Pine Hotel in Caliente! He'd been one of the raft of people who'd busted in with the Sheriff and stood around ah-ing and oh-ing. The man had guts. He'd come in while Healey and the girl were still warm to see what a neat job he'd done.

The traffic bell rang and I knew he'd recognized me, too. He went across that intersection like a bat out of hell, up Western to Fountain.

He lost us on Fountain. I talked to my driver like a father. I got down on my knees and begged him to keep that car in sight. I called him all the Portuguese pet-names I could think of and made up a few new ones, but Raines ran away from us on Fountain.

On the way back to the hotel I stopped at the Hollywood Branch of the Automobile Club and had a friend of mine look up the license number of the car. Of course it was the brother's car, in the brother's name. That didn't get me anywhere. I was pretty sure Raines wouldn't go back to his brother's place now that he knew I'd spotted him; and it was a cinch he wouldn't use that car very long.

He didn't know what I wanted. He might figure me for a dick and scram out of L A—out of the country. I sat in my room at the hotel and thought soft thoughts about what a chump I'd been not to go to him directly when he'd stopped with his brother in front of the Selwyn, and the speed of taxi-cabs as compared to automobiles—things like that. It looked like the Healey case was all washed up as far as I was concerned

I went out about five o'clock and walked. I walked down one side of Hollywood Boulevard to Bronson and back up the other side to Vine and went into the U Drive joint and rented the car again. I was nervous and jumpy and disgusted, and the best way for me to get over feeling that way is to drive it off.

I drove out through Cahuenga Pass a ways and then I had an idea and drove back to the Selwyn Apartments. The idea wasn't any good. William Raines told the clerk to send me up and he asked me what he could do for me and smiled and offered me a drink.

I said I wanted to get in touch with his brother on a deal that would do us both a lot of good. He said his brother was in Chicago and that he hadn't seen him for two years. I didn't tell him he was a liar. It wouldn't have done any good. I thanked him and went back down to the car.

I drove down to L A and had dinner in a Chinese place. Then I went back by the Santa Fe and found out about trains—I figured on going back to New York the next day.

On the way back to Hollywood I drove by the Garden Court. Not for any particular reason—I thought about Mrs Healey and it wasn't much out of the way.

The blue Chrysler was sitting squarely across the street from the entrance.

I parked up the street a little way and got out and went back to be sure. I lit a match and looked at the card on the steering column; the car was registered to another U Drive place, downtown, on South Hope.

I went across the street and walked by the desk with my nose in the air. The Spick elevator boy didn't even look at the folded bill I slipped him; he grinned self-consciously and said that a little red-haired man had gone up to four just a couple minutes ago. Mrs Healey was on four and there were only three apartments on a floor.

I listened at the door but could only hear a confused buzz that sounded like fast conversation. I turned the knob very slowly and put a little weight against the door. It was locked. I went down to the end of the hall and went out as quietly as possible through a double door to a fire-escape platform. By standing outside the railing and holding on with one hand and leaning far out I could see into the dining-room of Mrs Healey's apartment, could see a couple inches of the door that led, as well as I could remember, into the drawing-room. It was closed.

There is nothing that makes you feel quite so simple as hanging on a fire-escape, trying to look into a window. Particularly when you can't see anything through the window. After a few minutes I gave it up and climbed back over the railing.

I half sat on the railing and tried to figure things out. What business would the guy who shot Healey have with Mrs Healey? Did the blackmail angle that Raines and Mackay had hold over Healey cover Mrs Healey, too? Was Raines milking his lowdown for all it was worth? It was too deep for me.

I went back into the hall and listened at the door again. They were a little louder but not loud enough to do me any good. I went around a bend in the hall to what I figured to be the kitchen-door and gave it the slow turn and it opened. I mentally kicked myself for wasting time on the fire-escape, tiptoed into the dark kitchen and closed the door.

It suddenly occurred to me that I was in a quaint spot if somebody should come in. What the hell business did I have there! I fixed that, to myself, with some kind of vague slant about protecting Mrs Healey and edged over to the door, through to the room I'd been looking into from the fire-escape.

The door into the drawing-room was one of those paste-board arrangements that might just as well not be there. The first thing I heard was a small, suppressed scream like somebody had smacked a hand over somebody else's mouth, and then something like a piece of furniture being tipped over. It was a cinch someone was fighting in there, quietly—or as quietly as possible.

There wasn't much time to think about whether I was doing the right thing or not. If I'd thought about it I'd probably have been wrong, anyway. I turned the knob, swung the door open.

Mrs Healey was standing against the far wall. She was standing flat against the wall with one hand up to her mouth. Her eyes were very wide.

There were two men locked together on the floor near the central table and as I came in they rolled over a turn or so and one broke away and scrambled to his feet. It was Raines. He dived after a nickel-plated revolver that was lying on the floor on the far side of the table, and the other man, who had risen to his knees, dived after it, too. The other man was Gard.

He beat Raines by a hair but Raines was on his feet; he kicked the gun out of Gard's hand, halfway across the room. Gard grabbed his leg and pulled him down and they went round and round again. They fought very quietly; all you could hear was the sound of heavy breathing and an occasional bump.

I went over and picked up the gun and stooped over the mess of arms and legs and picked out Raines' red head and took hold of the barrel of the gun. I took dead aim and let Raines have it back of the ear. He relaxed.

Gard got up slowly. He ran his fingers through his hair and jiggled his shoulders around to straighten his coat and grinned foolishly.

I said: "Fancy, meeting you here."

I turned around and looked at Mrs Healey. She was still standing against the wall with her hand across her mouth. Then the ceiling fell down on top of my head and everything got dark very suddenly.

Darkness was around me when I opened my eyes, but I could see the outlines of a window and I could hear someone breathing somewhere near me. I don't know how long I was out. I sat up and my head felt like it was going to explode; I lay down again and closed my eyes.

After a while I tried it again and it was a little better. I crawled towards what I figured to be a door and ran into the wall and I got up on my feet and felt along the wall until I found the light switch.

Raines was lying in the same place I'd smacked him, but his hands and feet were tied with a length of clothes-line and there was a red, white and blue silk handkerchief jammed into his mouth. His eyes were open and he looked at me with an expression that I can only describe as bitter amusement.

Gard was lying belly-down on the floor near the door into the dining-room. He was the hard breather I'd heard in the darkness. He was still out.

I ungagged Raines and sat down. I kept having the feeling that my head was going to blow up. It was a very unpleasant feeling.

In a little while Raines got his jaws limbered up and started talking. The first thing he said was: "What a bright boy *you* turned out to be!" I was too sick to know very much about what that meant—or care.

He went on like that for some time, talking in a high, squeaky voice, and the idea gradually filtered through the large balloon-shaped ache that my head had turned into.

It seems that Raines and the Mackay gal had juggled Healey into a swell spot. One of their angles was that Healey, in an expansive moment, had entirely forgotten about Mrs Healey and married Miss Mackay. They had a lot of material besides; everything from the Mann Act to mayhem. When he'd made the hundred and fifty grand lick in Quebec they'd jumped him in Chicago.

Healey had ducked out of Chi and they'd tailed him, first to Salt Lake, then to Caliente. Monday night, Raines had helped Mackay put on the act in the hotel that Healey had told me about.

Raines hadn't got off the train with her or checked into the hotel with her because they didn't want to be seen together in case anything went wrong, but he ducked up that handy back stairway and they'd given Healey the act, showing him exactly the color and size of the spot they had him on.

Then, when Healey came down to my room, Raines had gone down and planted across the street in case Healey tried to powder.

Raines hadn't been there five minutes before Mrs Healey and a man rolled up in the blue Chrysler. Raines recognized Mrs Healey because she'd spotted Healey with Miss Mackay and Raines in a cabaret in Chicago once and crowned Miss Mackay with a beer bottle. It seems Mrs Healey was a nice quiet girl.

They parked in front of the hotel and the man went in a minute, probably to buy a cigar and get a peek at the register. Then he came out and talked to Mrs Healey a little while and went back in the little alleyway that led to the side door. He was only there a minute; he probably found out that it was practical to go into the hotel that way and came back and told her.

Along about that time in Raines' yarn I woke up to the fact that he was referring to the man who was with Mrs Healey as "this guy." I opened my eyes and looked at him and he was looking at Gard.

Gard had stayed in the car while Mrs Healey went back through the alleyway and into the hotel. After a couple minutes he got nervous and got out and walked up the street a little ways, and Raines went across the street and went upstairs to find out what it was all about. That must have been about the time I was checking out.

Gard must have been coming back down the other side of the street and he saw me come out and finagle with his car and get into mine, and he stayed away until hell started popping upstairs and I went into the hotel.

Raines stopped a minute. I got up and went over and rolled Gard over on his back. He groaned and opened his eyes and blinked up at me and then he sat up slowly and leaned against the wall.

Raines said Mrs Healey must have tried Healey's door and then waited till Healey came up the front stairway after he left me, and she ducked around a corner and watched Healey go into Mackay's room. By that time Raines was at the top of the back stairway and he watched Mrs Healey

61

take a gun out of her bag and go down and listen at Miss Mackay's door. When Healey opened the door after whittling Mackay, she backed him into the room and closed the door. Raines said she probably told him a few pertinent truths about himself and relieved him of what was left of the hundred and fifty and then opened him up with the .38.

It was a swell spot for her, with the Mackay gal there with a knife in her heart. Raines said he figured she'd intended to rub Healey from the start, before he could divorce her—Healey had said she'd sworn to kill him, before he left Chicago. A nice quiet girl—Mrs Healey. A lady.

She'd dodged Raines on the stairs and he'd chased her down to the car, but by that time Gard was back in the car with the engine running and they'd shoved off fast. Then Raines had come back up with the sheriff and his gang to look things over. That's where I'd seen him.

He'd taken the midnight train for L A and it had taken him all day Tuesday to locate Mrs Healey. He'd been putting the screws on her and Gard for a split of the important money and Gard had gone into a wrestling number with him just before I arrived.

By the time Raines had got all that out of his system Gard was sitting up straight with his mouth open and his hands moving around fast and that dumb, thoughtful look on his face as if he wanted to say something. When Raines stopped to breathe, Gard said that the lady had talked him into driving her up to Caliente because she said she was too nervous to wait for Healey in L A—she said she had to see Healey and try to make their scrap up right away, or she'd have a nervous breakdown or something and Gard—the big chump—fell for it.

He said he was the most surprised man in the world when the shooting started, and that when she came galloping down and they scrammed for L A she'd told him that she'd walked in on Mackay ventilating Healey, just like the sheriff said, and that Mackay had shot at her as she ran away. Gard had fallen for that, too. She had the poor sap hypnotized.

Gard knew I'd been up at Caliente, of course—he'd seen me; so when I walked into his place in the morning he'd figured I had some kind of slant on what it was all about and he'd taken me over to her place so they could put on their "comfort her in her bereavement" turn for my benefit.

Then, Tuesday night, when I'd walked in on the shakedown and knocked Raines out, Gard, who had had a load of what Raines had to say to Mrs Healey and who half believed it, calculated that his best play was to take the air with her. He was too much mixed up in it to beat an accessory rap anyway, so he'd sapped me with a bookend and they'd tied Raines, who was coming to, and he'd helped her pack her things. They were going to light out for New Zealand or some quiet place like that; only she'd sneaked up behind him and smacked him down at the last minute. A lovely lady.

We all stopped talking about that time—Raines and Gard and me—and looked at one another.

Gard laughed. He squinted at me and said: "You looked silly when I clipped you with the bookend!"

Raines said: "You didn't look particularly intelligent when our girl-friend let *you* have it."

Gard snickered on the wrong side of his face and got up and went out into the kitchen for a drink of water. He found a bottle out there—almost a full fifth of White Horse. He brought it in, I untied Raines and we all had a snort.

I was thinking about what suckers we'd been. I'd popped Raines and Gard had popped me and Mrs Healey had popped Gard—all of us. One, two, three. Tinker to Evers to Chance—only more so.

I think we were all pretty washed up with La Belle Healey. It was a cinch Gard wouldn't want any more of her. I don't know about Raines, but I know I didn't.

We finished the bottle and Raines snooped around and found a full one and we did a little business with that.

I didn't find out I had a concussion till next morning. I was a week and two days in the hospital at twenty dollars a day, and the doctor nicked me two-fifty. He'll get the rest of it when he catches me.

The whole Healey play, what with one thing and another, cost somewhere in the neighborhood of a grand. I got a lame skull and about two-bits' worth of fun out of it.

I pass.

Coleman said: "Eight ball in the corner."

There was soft click of ball against ball and then sharper click as the black ball dropped into the pocket Coleman had called.

Coleman put his cue in the rack. He rolled down the sleeves of his vividly striped silk shirt and put on his coat and a pearl gray velour hat. He went to the pale fat man who slouched against a neighboring table and took two crisp hundred dollar notes from the fat man's outstretched hand, glanced at the slim, pimpled youth who had been his opponent, smiled thinly, said: "So long," went to the door, out into the street.

There was sudden roar from a black, curtained roadster on the other side of the street; the sudden ragged roar of four or five shots close together, a white pulsing finger of flame in the dusk, and Coleman sank to his knees. He swayed backwards once, fell forward onto his face hard; his gray hat rolled slowly across the sidewalk. The roadster was moving, had disappeared before Coleman was entirely still. It became very quiet in the street.

Mazie Decker curved her orange mouth to its best "Customer" smile. She took the little green ticket that the dark-haired boy held out to her and tore off one corner and dropped the rest into the slot. He took her tightly in his arms and as the violins melted to sound and the lights dimmed they swung out across the crowded floor.

Her head was tilted back, her bright mouth near the blue smoothness of his jaw.

She whispered: "Gee—I didn't think you was coming."

He twisted his head down a little, smiled at her.

She spoke again without looking at him: "I waited till one o'clock for you last night." She hesitated a moment then went on rapidly: "Gee—I act like I'd known you for years, an' it's only two days. What a sap I turned out to be!" She giggled mirthlessly.

He didn't answer.

The music swelled to brassy crescendo, stopped. They stood with a hundred other couples and applauded mechanically.

She said: "Gee—I love a waltz! Don't you?"

He nodded briefly and as the orchestra bellowed to a moaning foxtrot he took her again in his arms and they circled towards the far end of the floor.

"Let's get out of here, kid." He smiled to a thin line against the whiteness of his skin, his large eyes half closed.

She said: "All right—only let's try to get out without the manager seeing me. I'm supposed to work till eleven."

They parted at one of the little turnstiles; he got his hat and coat from the check-room, went downstairs and got his car from a parking station across the street.

When she came down he had double-parked near the entrance. He honked his horn and held the door open for her as she trotted breathlessly out and climbed in beside him. Her eyes were very bright and she laughed a little hysterically.

"The manager saw me," she said. "But I said I was sick— an' it worked." She snuggled up close to him as he swung the car into Sixth Street. "Gee—what a swell car!"

He grunted affirmatively and they went out Sixth a block or so in silence.

As they turned north on Figueroa she said: "What've you got the side curtains on for? It's such a beautiful night."

He offered her a cigarette and lighted one for himself and leaned back comfortably in the seat.

He said: "I think it's going to rain."

It was very dark at the side of the road. A great pepper tree screened the roadster from whatever light there was in the sky.

Mazie Decker spoke softly: "Angelo. Angelo—that's a beautiful name. It sounds like angel."

The dark youth's face was hard in the narrow glow of the dashlight. He had taken off his hat and his shiny black hair looked like a metal skullcap. He stroked the heel of his

66

hand back over one ear, over the oily blackness and then he took his hand down and wriggled it under his coat. His other arm was around the girl.

He took his hand out of the darkness of his coat and there was brief flash of bright metal; the girl said: "My God!" slowly and put her hands up to her breast. . . .

He leaned in front of her and pressed the door open and as her body sank into itself he pushed her gently and her body slanted, toppled through the door, fell softly on the leaves beside the road. Her sharp breath and a far quavering "Ah!" were blotted out as he pressed the starter and the motor roared; he swung the door closed and put on his hat carefully, shifted gears and let the clutch in slowly.

As he came out of the darkness of the dirt road on to the highway he thrust one hand through a slit in the side-curtain, took it in and leaned forward over the wheel.

It was raining, a little.

R. F. Winfield stretched one long leg out and planted his foot on a nearby leather chair. The blonde woman got up and walked unsteadily to the phonograph. This latter looked like a grandfather clock, had cost well into four figures, would probably have collapsed at the appellation "phonograph"—but it was.

The blonde woman snapped the little tin brake; she lifted the record, stared empty-eyed at the other side.

She said: " 's Minnie th' Moocher. Wanna hear it?"

Mr Winfield said: "Uh-huh." He tilted an ice and amber filled glass to his mouth, drained it. He stood up and gathered his very blue dressing-gown about his lean shanks. He lifted his head and walked through a short corridor to the bathroom, opened the door, entered.

Water splashed noisily in the big blue porcelain tub. He braced himself with one hand on the shower-tap, turned off the water, slipped out of the dressing-gown and into the tub.

The blonde woman's voice clanged like cold metal through the partially open door.

"Took 'er down to Chinatown; showed 'er how to kick the gong aroun'."

Mr Winfield reached up into the pocket of the

dressing-gown, fished out a cigarette, matches. He lighted the cigarette, leaned back in the water, sighed. His face was a long tan oblong of contentment. He flexed his jaw, then mechanically put up one hand and removed an upper plate, put the little semi-circle of shining teeth on the basin beside the tub, ran his tongue over thick, sharply etched lips, sighed again. The warm water was soft, caressing; he was very comfortable.

He heard the buzzer and he heard the blonde woman stagger along the corridor past the bathroom to the outer door of the apartment. He listened but could hear no word of anything said there; only the sound of the door opening and closing, and silence broken faintly by the phonograph's "Hi-de-ho-oh, Minnie."

Then the bathroom door swung slowly open and a man stood outlined against the darkness of the corridor. He was bareheaded and the electric light was reflected in a thin line across his hair, shone dully on the moist pallor of his skin. He wore a tightly belted raincoat and his hands were thrust deep into his pockets.

Winfield sat up straight in the tub, spoke tentatively "Hello!" He said "hello" with an incredulous rising inflection, blinked incredulously upward. The cigarette dangled loosely from one corner of his mouth.

The man leaned against the frame of the door and took a short thick automatic out of his coat pocket and held it steadily, waist high.

Winfield put his hands on the sides of the tub and started to get up.

The automatic barked twice.

Winfield half stood, with one hand and one leg braced against the side of the tub for perhaps five seconds. His eyes were wide, blank. Then he sank down slowly, his head fell back against the smooth blue porcelain, slid slowly under the water. The cigarette still hung in the corner of his clenched mouth and as his head went under the water it hissed briefly, was gone.

The man in the doorway turned, disappeared.

The water reddened. Faintly, the phonograph lisped: "Hi de ho. . . ."

* * * * *

Doolin grinned up at the waiter. "An' see the eggs are four minutes, an' don't put any cream in my coffee."

The waiter bobbed his head sullenly and disappeared through swinging doors.

Doolin unfolded his paper and turned to the comic page. He read it carefully, chuckling audibly, from top to bottom. Then he spread pages two and three across the counter and began at the top of page two. Halfway across he read the headline: Winfield, Motion Picture Executive, Slain by Sweetheart: Story continued from page one.

He turned to the front page and stared at a two-column cut of Winfield, read the accompanying account, turned back to page two and finished it. There was another cut of Winfield, and a woman. The caption under the woman's picture read: "Elma O'Shea Darmond, well-known screen actress and friend of Winfield, who was found unconscious in his apartment with the automatic in her hand."

Doolin yawned and shoved the paper aside to make room for the eggs and toast and coffee that the sour-faced waiter carried. He devoured the eggs and had half-finished his coffee before he saw something that interested him on page three. He put his cup down, leaned over the paper, read: "Man shot in Glendale Mystery. H J (Jake) Coleman, alleged gambler, was shot and killed as he came out of the Lyric Billiard Parlors in Glendale yesterday evening. The shots were fired from a mysterious black roadster which the police are attempting to trace."

Doolin read the rest of the story, finished his coffee. He sat several minutes staring expressionlessly at his reflection in the mirror behind the counter, got up, paid his check and went out into the bright morning.

He walked briskly down Hill Street to First, over First, to the Los Angeles Bulletin Building. He was whistling as the elevator carried him up.

In the back files of the *Bulletin* he found what he was looking for, a front-page spread in the Home Edition of December 10th:

MASSACRE IN NIGHTCLUB
Screen-stars Duck for Cover as Machine-guns Belch Death

Early this morning The Hotspot, famous cabaret near Culver City, was the scene of the bloodiest battle the local gang war has afforded to date. Two men who police believe to be Frank Riccio and Edward (Whitey) Conroy of the Purple Gang in Detroit were instantly killed when a private room in the club was invaded by four men with sub-machine guns. A third man, a companion of Riccio and Conroy, was seriously wounded and is not expected to live.

Doolin skimmed down the column, read:

R. F. Winfield, prominent motion-picture executive, who was one of the party in the private room, said that he could not identify any of the killers. He said it all happened too quickly to be sure of any of them, and explained his presence in the company of the notorious gangsters as the result of his desire for first-hand information about the underworld in connection with a picture of that type which he is supervising. The names of others in the party are being withheld. . . .

Under a sub-head Doolin read:

H. J. Coleman and his companion, Miss Mazie Decker, were in the corridor leading to the private room when the killers entered. Miss Decker said she could positively identify two of them. Coleman, who is near-sighted, was equally positive that he could not. . . .

An hour and a half later, Doolin left the Bulletin Building. He had gone carefully through the December file, and up to the middle of January. He had called into service the City Directory, telephone book, Dun & Bradstreet, and the telephone, and he had wheedled all the inside dope he could out of a police-reporter whom he knew casually.

He stood on the wide stone steps and looked at the sheet of paper on which he had scrawled notes. It read:

People in private room and corridor who might be able to identify killers of Riccio and Conroy:
Winfield. Dead.

70

Coleman. Dead.

Martha Grainger. Actress. In show, in N. Y.

Betty Crane. Hustler. Died of pneumonia January 4th.

Isabel Dolly. Hustler and extra-girl. Was paralyzed drunk during shooting; probably not important. Can't locate.

Mazie Decker. Taxi-dancer. Works at Dreamland on Sixth and Hill. Failed to identify killers from rogues-gallery photographs.

Nelson Halloran. Man-about-town. Money. Friend of Winfield's. Lives at Fontenoy, same apartment-house as Winfield.

Doolin folded and creased the sheet of paper. He wound it abstractedly around his forefinger and walked down the steps, across the sidewalk to a cab. He got into the cab and sat down and leaned back.

The driver slid the glass, asked: "Where to?"

Doolin stared at him blankly, then laughed. He said: "Wait a minute," spread the sheet of paper across his knee. He took a stub of pencil out of his pocket and slowly, thoughtfully, drew a line through the first five names; that left Mazie Decker and Nelson Halloran.

Doolin leaned forward and spoke to the driver: "Is that Dreamland joint at Sixth an' Hill open in the afternoon?"

The driver thought a moment, shook his head.

Doolin said: "All right, then—Fontenoy Apartments—on Whitley in Hollywood."

Nelson Halloran looked like Death. His white face was extremely long, narrow; his sharp chin tapered upward in unbroken lines to high sharp cheek-bones, great deep-sunken eyes; continued to a high, almost degenerately narrow, forehead. His mouth was wide, thin, dark against the whiteness of his skin. His hair was the color of water. He was six-feet-three inches tall, weighed a hundred and eighty.

He half lay in a deeply upholstered chair in the living room of his apartment and watched a round spot of sunlight move across the wall. The shades were drawn and the apartment was in semi-darkness. It was a chaos of modern furniture, books, magazines, papers, bottles; there were several good but badly hung reproductions on the pale walls.

Halloran occasionally lifted one long white hand languidly to his mouth, inhaled smoke deeply and blew it upward into the ray of sunlight.

When the phone buzzed he shuddered involuntarily, leaned sidewise and took it up from a low table.

He listened a moment, said: "Send him up." His voice was very low. There was softness in it; and there was coldness and something very far-away.

He moved slightly in the chair so that one hand was near his side, in the folds of his dressing gown. There was a Luger there in the darkness of the chair. He was facing the door.

With the whirl of the buzzer he called: "Come in."

The door opened and Doolin came a little way into the room, closed the door behind him.

Halloran did not speak.

Doolin stood blinking in the half-light, and Halloran watched him and was silent.

Doolin was around thirty; of medium height, inclined to thickness through all the upper part of his body. His face was round and on the florid side and his eyes were wide-set, blue. His clothes didn't fit him very well.

He stood with his hat in his hand, his face expressionless, until Halloran said coldly: "I didn't get the name."

"Doolin. D—double o-l-i-n." Doolin spoke without moving his mouth very much. His voice was pleasant; his vowels colored slightly by brogue.

Halloran waited.

Doolin said: "I read a couple of things in the paper this morning that gave me an idea. I went over to the *Bulletin* an' worked on the idea, an' it pans out you're in a very bad spot."

Halloran took a drag of his cigarette, stared blankly at Doolin, waited. Doolin waited, too. They were both silent, looking at one another for more than a minute. Doolin's eyes were bright, pleased.

Halloran finally said: "This is a little embarrassing." He hesitated a moment. "Sit down."

Doolin sat on the edge of a wide steel and canvas chair against the wall. He dropped his hat on the floor and leaned forward, put his elbows on his knees. The little circle of sunlight moved slowly across the wall above him.

Halloran mashed his cigarette out, changed his position a little, said: "Go on."

"Have you read the papers?" Doolin took a cellophane-wrapped cigar out of his pocket and ripped off the wrapper, clamped the cigar between his teeth.

Halloran nodded, if moving his head the merest fraction of an inch could be called a nod.

Doolin spoke around the cigar: "Who rubbed Riccio and Conroy?"

Halloran laughed.

Doolin took the cigar out of his mouth. He said very earnestly: "Listen. Last night Winfield was murdered—an' Coleman. You're next. I don't know why the people who did it waited so long—maybe because the trial of a couple of the boys they've been holding comes up next week. . . ."

Halloran's face was a blank white mask.

Doolin leaned back and crossed his legs. "Anyway—they got Winfield an' Coleman. That leaves the Decker broad—the one who was with Coleman—an' you. The rest of them don't count—one's in New York an' one died of pneumonia an, one was cockeyed. . . ."

He paused to chew his cigar, Halloran rubbed his left hand down over one side of his face, slowly.

Doolin went on: "I used to be a stunt-man in pictures. For the last year all the breaks have been bad. I haven't worked for five months." He leaned forward, emphasized his words with the cigar held like a pencil: "I want to work for you."

There was thin amusement in Halloran's voice: "What are your qualifications?"

"I can shoot straight, an' fast, an' I ain't afraid to take a chance—any kind of a chance! I'd make a hell of a swell bodyguard."

Doolin stood up in the excitement of his sales-talk, took two steps towards Halloran.

Halloran said: "Sit down." His voice was icy. The Luger glistened in his hand.

Doolin looked at the gun and smiled a little, stuck the cigar in his mouth and backed up and sat down.

Halloran said: "How am I supposed to know you're on the level?"

Doolin slid his lower lip up over the upper. He scratched his nose with the nail of his thumb and shook his head slowly, grinning.

73

"Anyway—it sounds like a pipe dream to me," Halloran went on. "The paper says Miss Darmond killed Winfield." He smiled. "And Coleman was a gambler—any one of a half dozen suckers is liable to have shot him."

Doolin shrugged elaborately. He leaned forward and picked up his hat and put it on, stood up.

Halloran laughed again. His laugh was not a particularly pleasing one.

"Don't be in a hurry," he said.

They were silent a while and then Halloran lighted a cigarette and stood up. He was so tall and spare that Doolin stared involuntarily as he crossed, holding the Luger loosely at his side, patted Doolin's pockets, felt under his arms with his free hand. Then Halloran went to a table across a corner of the room and dropped the Luger into a drawer.

He turned and smiled warmly at Doolin, said: "What will you drink?"

"Gin."

"No gin."

Doolin grinned.

Halloran went on: "Scotch, rye, bourbon, brandy, rum, Kirsch, champagne. No gin."

Doolin said: "Rye."

Halloran took two bottles from a tall cabinet, poured two drinks. "Why don't you go to the Decker girl? She's the one who said she could identify the men who killed Riccio and Conroy. She's the one who needs a bodyguard."

Doolin went over to the table and picked up his drink. "I ain't had a chance," he said. "She works at Dreamland downtown, an' it ain't open in the afternoon." They drank.

Halloran's mouth was curved to a small smile. He picked up a folded newspaper, pointed to a headline, handed it to Doolin.

Doolin took the paper, a late edition of the *Morning Bulletin*, read:

**MURDERED GIRL
IDENTIFIED AS
TAXI-DANCER**

The body of the girl who was found stabbed to death

74

on the road near Lankershim early this morning, has been identified as Mazie Decker of 305 S. Lake Street, an employee of the Dreamland Dancing Studio.

The identification was made by Peggy Galbraith, the murdered girl's room-mate. Miss Decker did not return home last night, and upon reading an account of the tragedy in the early editions, Miss Galbraith went to the morgue and positively identified Miss Decker. The police are . . .

Doolin put the paper down, said: "Well, well. . . . Like I said. . . ." There was a knock at the door, rather a curious rhythmic tapping of fingernails.

Halloran called: "Come in."

The door opened and a woman came in slowly, closed the door. She went to Halloran and put her arms around him and tilted her head back.

Halloran kissed her lightly. He smiled at Doolin, said: "This is Mrs Sare." He turned his smile to the woman. "Lola—meet Mr Doolin—my bodyguard."

Lola Sare had no single feature, except her hair, that was beautiful; yet she was very beautiful.

Her hair was red, so dark that it was black in certain lights. Her eyes slanted; were so dark a green they were usually black. Her nose was straight but the nostrils flared the least bit too much; her mouth red and full; too wide and curved. Her skin was smooth, very dark. Her figure was good, on the slender side. She was ageless; perhaps twenty-six, perhaps thirty-six.

She wore a dark green robe of heavy silk, black mules; her hair was gathered in a large roll at the nape of her neck.

She inclined her head sharply towards Doolin, without expression.

Doolin said: "Very happy to know you, Mrs Sare."

She went to one of the wide windows and jerked the drape aside a little; a broad flat beam of sunshine yellowed the darkness.

She said: "Sorry to desecrate the tomb." Her voice was deep, husky.

Halloran poured three drinks and went back to his chair

and sat down. Mrs Sare leaned against the table, and Doolin, after a hesitant glance at her, sat down on the chair against the wall.

Halloran sipped his drink. "The strange part of it all," he said, "is that I couldn't identify any of the four men who came in that night if my life depended upon it—and I'm almost sure Winfield couldn't. We'd been on a bender together for three days—and my memory for faces is bad, at best. . . ."

He put his glass on the floor beside the chair, lighted a cigarette. "Who else did you mention, besides the Decker girl and Coleman and Winfield and myself, who might . . . ?"

Doolin took the folded sheet of paper out of his pocket, got up and handed it to Halloran.

Halloran studied it a while, said: "You missed one."

Mrs Sare picked up the two bottles and went to Doolin, refilled his glass.

Doolin stared questioningly at Halloran, his eyebrows raised to a wide inverted V.

"The man who was with Riccio and Conroy," Halloran went on. "The third man, who was shot. . . ."

Doolin said: "I didn't see any more about him in the files—the paper said he wasn't expected to live. . . ."

Halloran clicked the nail of his forefinger against his teeth, said: "I wonder."

Mrs Sare had paused to listen. She went to Halloran and refilled his glass and put the bottles on the floor, sat down on the arm of Halloran's chair.

"Winfield and I went to The Hotspot alone," Halloran went on. "We had some business to talk over with a couple girls in the show." He grinned faintly, crookedly at Mrs Sare. "Riccio and Conroy and this third man—I think his name was Martini or something dry like that—and the three girls on your list, passed our table on their way to the private-room. . . ."

Doolin was leaning forward, chewing his cigar, his eyes bright with interest.

Halloran blew smoke up into the wedge of sun. "Winfield knew Conroy casually—had met him in the East. They fell on one another's necks, and Conroy invited us to join their party. Winfield went for that—he was doing a gangster picture and Conroy was a big shot in the East—Winfield figured he could get a lot of angles. . . ."

Doolin said: "That was on the level, then?"

"Yes," Halloran nodded emphatically. "Winfield even talked of making Conroy technical expert on the picture—before the fireworks started."

"What did this third man—this Martini, look like?"

Halloran looked a little annoyed. He said: "I'll get to that. There were eight of us in the private room—the three men and the three girls and Winfield and I. Riccio was pretty drunk, and one of the girls was practically under the table. We were all pretty high."

Halloran picked up his glass, leaned forward. "Riccio and Martini were all tangled up in some kind of drunken argument and I got the idea it had something to do with drugs—morphine. Riccio was pretty loud. Winfield and I were talking to Conroy, and the girls were amusing themselves gargling champagne, when the four men—I guess there were four—crashed in and opened up on Riccio and Conroy. . . ."

"What about Martini?" Doolin's unlighted cigar was growing rapidly shorter.

Halloran looked annoyed again. "That's the point," he said. "They didn't pay any attention to Martini—they wanted Riccio and Conroy. And it wasn't machine-guns—that was newspaper color. It was automatics. . . ."

Doolin said: "What about Martini?"

"For Christ's sake—shut up!" Halloran grinned cheerlessly, finished his drink. "Riccio shot Martini."

Doolin stood up slowly, said: "Can I use the phone?"

Halloran smiled at Mrs Sare, nodded.

Doolin called several numbers, asked questions, said "Yes" and "No" monotonously.

Halloran and Mrs Sare talked quietly. Between two calls, Halloran spoke to Doolin: "You've connections—haven't you." It was an observation, not a question.

Doolin said: "If I had as much money as I have connections, I'd retire."

He finished after a while, hung up and put the phone back on the low round-table.

"Martinelli," he said, "not Martini. Supposed to have been Riccio and Conroy's partner in the East. They had the

77

drug business pretty well cornered. He showed up out here around the last of November, and Riccio and Conroy came in December tenth, were killed the night they got in. . . ."

Halloran said: "I remember that—they were talking about the trip."

Doolin took the cigar out of his mouth long enough to take a drink. "Martinelli was discharged from St. Vincent's Hospital January sixteenth—day before yesterday. He's plenty bad—beat four or five murder raps in the East and was figured for a half dozen others. They called him The Executioner. Angelo Martinelli—The Executioner."

Mrs Sare said: "Come and get it."

Doolin and Halloran got up and went into the little dining room. They sat down at the table and Mrs Sare brought in a steaming platter of bacon and scrambled eggs, a huge double-globe of bubbling coffee.

Doolin said: "Here's the way it looks to me: If Martinelli figured you an' Winfield an' whoever else was in the private room had seen Riccio shoot him, he'd want to shut you up; it was a cinch he'd double-crossed Riccio and if it came out at the trial, the Detroit boys would be on his tail."

Halloran nodded, poured a large rosette of chili-sauce on the plate beside his scrambled eggs.

"But what did he want to rub Coleman an' Decker for?"

Halloran started to speak with his mouth full, but Doolin interrupted him: "The answer to that is that Martinelli had hooked up with the outfit out here, the outfit that Riccio and Conroy figured on moving in on. . . ."

Halloran said: "Martinelli probably came out to organize things for a narcotic combination between here and Detroit, in opposition to our local talent. He liked the combination here the way it was and threw in with them—and when Riccio and Conroy arrived Martinelli put the finger on them, for the local boys. . . ."

Doolin swallowed a huge mouthful of bacon and eggs, said: "Swell," out of the corner of his mouth to Mrs Sare.

He picked up his cigar and pointed it at Halloran. "That's the reason he wanted all of you—you an' Winfield because you'd get the Detroit outfit on his neck if you testified; Decker an' Coleman because they could spot the L A boys.

He didn't try to proposition any of you—he's the kind of guy who would figure killing was simpler."

Halloran said: "He's got to protect himself against the two men who are in jail too. They're liable to spill their guts. If everybody who was in on it was bumped there wouldn't be a chance of those two guys being identified—everything would be rosy."

They finished their bacon and eggs in silence.

With the coffee, Doolin said: "Funny he didn't make a pass at you last night—before or after he got Winfield. The same building an' all. . . ."

"Maybe he did." Halloran put his arm around Mrs Sare who was standing beside his chair. "I didn't get home till around three—he was probably here, missed me."

Doolin said: "We better go downtown an' talk to the D A. That poor gal of Winfield's is probably on the grill. We can clear that up an' have Martinelli picked up. . . ."

Halloran said: "No." He said it very emphatically.

Doolin opened his eyes wide, slowly. He finished his coffee, waited.

Halloran smiled faintly, said: "In the first place, I hate coppers." He tightened his arm around Mrs Sare. "In the second place I don't particularly care for Miss Darmond—she can God damned well fry on the griddle from now on, so far as I'm concerned. In the third place—I like it. . . ."

Doolin glanced at Mrs Sare, turned his head slowly back towards Halloran.

"I've got three months to live," Halloran went on—"at the outside." His voice was cold, entirely unemotional. "I was shell-shocked and gassed and kicked around pretty generally in France in 'eighteen. They stuck me together and sent me back and I've lasted rather well. But my heart is shot, and my lungs are bad, and so on—the doctors are getting pretty sore because I'm still on my feet. . . ."

He grinned widely. "I'm going to have all the fun I can in whatever time is left. We're not going to call copper, and we're going to play this for everything we can get out of it. You're my bodyguard and your salary is five hundred a week, but your job isn't to guard me—it's to see that there's plenty of excitement. And instead of waiting for Martinelli to come to us, we're going to Martinelli."

Doolin looked blankly at Mrs Sare. She was smiling in a very curious way.

Halloran said: "Are you working?"

Doolin smiled slowly with all his face. He said: "Sure."

Doolin dried his hands and smoothed his hair, whistling tunelessly, went through the small cheaply furnished living room of his apartment to the door of the kitchenette. He picked up a newspaper from a table near the door, unfolded it and glanced at the headlines, said: "They're calling the Winfield kill 'Murder in Blue' because it happened in a blue bathtub. Is that a laugh!"

A rather pretty fresh-faced girl was stirring something in a white sauce-pan on the little gas stove. She looked up and smiled and said: "Dinner'll be ready in a minute," wiped her hands on her apron and began setting the table.

Doolin leaned against the wall and skimmed through the rest of the paper. The Coleman case was limited to a quarter column—the police had been unable to trace the car. There was even less about Mazie Decker. The police were "working on a theory. . . ."

The police were working on a theory, too, on the Winfield killing. Miss Darmond had been found near the door of Winfield's apartment with a great bruise on her head, the night of the murder; she said the last she remembered was opening the door and struggling with someone. The "Best Minds" of the Force believed her story up to that point; they were working on the angle that she had an accomplice.

Doolin rolled up the paper and threw it on a chair. He said: "Five hundred a week—an' expenses! Gee!—is that swell!" He was grinning broadly.

The girl said: "I'm awfully glad about the money, darling—if you're SURE you'll be safe. God knows it's about time we had a break." She hesitated a moment. "I hope it's all right. . . ."

She was twenty-three or four, a honey-blonde pink-cheeked girl with wide gray eyes, a slender well-curved figure.

Doolin went to her and kissed the back of her neck.

"Sure, it's all right, Mollie," he said. "Anything is all right when you get paid enough for it. The point is to make it last—five hundred is a lot of money, but a thousand will buy twice as many lamb chops."

She became very interested in a tiny speck on one of the cheap white plates, rubbed it industriously with a towel. She spoke without looking up: "I keep thinking about that Darmond girl—in jail. What do you suppose Halloran has against her?"

"I don't know." Doolin sat down at the table. "Anyway—she's okay. We can spring her any time, only we can't do it now because we'd have to let the Law in on the Martinelli angle an' they'd pick him up—an' Halloran couldn't have his fun."

"It's a funny kind of fun." The girl smiled with her mouth.

Doolin said: "He's a funny guy. Used to be a police reporter in Chi—maybe that has something to do with it. Anyway, the poor bastard's only got a little while to go—let him have any kind of fun he wants. He can afford it. . . ."

They were silent while the girl cut bread and got the butter out of the Frigidaire and finished setting the table.

Doolin was leaning forward with his elbows on the table, his chin in his hands. "As far as the Darmond gal is concerned, a little of that beef stew they dish up at the County will be good for her. These broads need a little of that—to give them perspective."

The girl was heaping mashed potatoes into a big bowl. She did not speak.

"The way I figure it," Doolin went on—"Halloran hasn't got the guts to bump himself off. He's all washed up, an' he knows it—an' the idea has made him a little batty. Then along comes Martinelli—a chance for him to go out dramatically—the way he's lived—an' he goes for it. Jesus! so would I if I was as near the edge as he is. He doesn't give a god-damn about anything—he doesn't have to. . . ."

The girl finished putting food on the table, sat down. Doolin heaped their plates with chops and potatoes and cauliflower while she served salad. They began to eat.

Doolin got up and filled two glasses with water and put them on the table.

The girl said: "I'm sorry I forgot the water. . . ."

Doolin bent over and kissed her, sat down.

"As far as Halloran is concerned," he went on—"I'm just another actor in his show. Instead of sitting and waiting for Martinelli to come to get him—we go after Martinelli. That's Halloran's idea of fun—that's the kind of sense of humor he's got. What the hell!—he's got nothing to lose. . . ."

The girl said: "Eat your dinner before it gets cold."

They were silent a while.

Finally she said: "What if Martinelli shoots first?"

Doolin laughed. "Martinelli isn't going to shoot at all. Neither am I—an' neither is Mr Halloran."

The girl lighted a cigarette, sipped her coffee. She stared expressionlessly at Doolin, waited.

"Halloran is having dinner with Mrs Sare," Doolin went on. "Then they're going to a show an' I'm picking them up afterwards—at the theatre. Then Halloran an' I are going to have a look around for Martinelli."

He finished his coffee, refilled both their cups. "In the meantime I'm supposed to be finding out where we're most likely to find him—Halloran is a great believer in my 'connections.' "

Doolin grinned, went on with a softly satisfied expression, as if he were taking a rabbit out of a hat: "I've already found Martinelli—not only where he hangs out, but where he lives. It was a cinch. He hasn't any reason to think he's pegged for anything—he's not hiding out."

The girl said: "So what?"

He stood up, stretched luxuriously. "So I'm going to Martinelli right now." He paused dramatically. "An' I'm going to tell him what kind of a spot he's in—with half a dozen murder raps hanging over his head, and all. I'm going to tell him that plenty people besides myself know about it an' that the stuff's on the way to the D A's office an' that he'd better scram toot sweet. . . ."

The girl said: "You're crazy."

Doolin laughed extravagantly. "Like a fox," he said. "Like a fox. I'm doing Martinelli a big favor—so I'm set with him. I'm keeping Halloran from running a chance of being killed—an' he'll think he's still running the chance, an' get his throb out of it. I'm keeping five hundred smackers coming into the cash register every week as long as Halloran lives, or as long as I can give him a good show. An' everybody's happy. What more do you want?"

"Sense." The girl mashed her cigarette out, stood up. "I never heard such a crazy idea in all my life! . . ."

Doolin looked disgusted. He walked into the living room, came back to the doorway. "Sure, it's crazy," he said. "Sure, it's crazy. So is Halloran—an' you—an' me. So is Martinelli—probably. It's the crazy ideas that work—an' this one is going to work like a charm."

The girl said: "What about Darmond? If Martinelli gets away she'll be holding the bag for Winfield's murder."

"Oh, no, she won't! As soon as the Halloran angle washes up I'll turn my evidence over to the D A an' tell him it took a few weeks to get it together—an' be sure about it. It's as plain as the nose on your face that Martinelli killed all three of them. Those chumps downtown are too sappy to see it now but they won't be when I point it out to them. It's a set-up case against Martinelli!"

The girl smiled coldly. She said: "You're the most conceited, bull-headed Mick that ever lived. You've been in one jam after another ever since we were married. This is one time I'm not going to let you make a fool of yourself—an' probably get killed. . . ."

Doolin's expression was stubborn, annoyed. He turned and strode across the living room, squirmed into his coat, put on his hat and jerked it down over his eyes.

She stood in the doorway. Her face was very white and her eyes were wide, round.

She said: "Please. Johnny. . . ."

He didn't look at her. He went to the desk against one wall and opened a drawer, took a nickel-plated revolver out of the drawer and dropped it into his coat pocket.

She said: "If you do this insane thing—I'm leaving." Her voice was cold, brittle.

Doolin went to the outer-door, went out, slammed the door.

She stood there a little while looking at the door.

Angelo Martinelli stuck two fingers of his left hand into the little jar, took them out pale, green, sticky with Smoothcomb Hair Dressing. He dabbed it on his head, held his hands stiff with the fingers bent backwards and rubbed it vigorously into his hair. Then he wiped his hands and picked up a comb, bent towards the mirror.

Martinelli was very young—perhaps twenty-four or -five. His face was pale, unlined; pallor shading to blue towards his long angular jaw; his eyes red-brown, his nose straight and delicately cut. He was of medium height but the high padded shoulders of his coat made him appear taller.

The room was small, garishly furnished. A low bed and two or three chairs in the worst modern manner were made a little more objectionable by orange and pink batik throws; there was an elaborately wrought iron floor lamp, its shade made of whiskey labels pasted on imitation parchment.

Martinelli finished combing his hair, spoke over his shoulder to a woman who lounged across the foot of the bed:

"Tonight does it. . . ."

Lola Sare said: "Tonight does it—if you're careful. . . ."

Martinelli glanced at his wrist-watch. "I better get going—it's nearly eight. He said he'd be there at eight."

Lola Sare leaned forward and dropped her cigarette into a half-full glass on the floor.

"I'll be home from about eight-thirty on," she said. "Call as soon as you can."

Martinelli nodded. He put on a lightweight black felt hat, tilted it to the required angle in front of the mirror. He helped her into her coat, and then he put his arms around her, kissed her mouth lingeringly.

She clung to him, whispered: "Make it as fast as you can, darling."

They went to the door and Martinelli snapped off the light and they went out.

Martinelli said: "Turn right at the next corner."

The cab driver nodded; they turned off North Broadway into a dimly lighted street, went several blocks over bad pavement.

Martinelli pounded on the glass, said: "Oke."

The cab slid to an abrupt stop and Martinelli got out and paid the driver, stood at the curb until the cab had turned around in the narrow street, disappeared.

He went to a door above which one pale electric globe

glittered, felt in the darkness for the button, pressed it. The door clicked open; Martinelli went in and slammed it shut behind him.

There were a half dozen or so men strung out along the bar in the long dim room. A few more sat at tables against the wall.

Martinelli walked to the far end of the bar, leaned across it to speak quietly to a chunky bald-headed man who sat on a high stool near the cash register:

"Chief here?"

The bald man bobbed his head, jerked it towards a door behind Martinelli.

Martinelli looked surprised, said mildly: "He's on time for once in his life!"

The man bobbed his head. His face was blank.

Martinelli went through the door, up two short flights of stairs to a narrow hallway. At the end of the hallway he knocked at a heavy steel-sheathed fire-door.

After a little while the door opened and a voice said: "Come in."

Doolin stood on his toes and tried to make out the number above the door but the figures were too faded by weather, time; the electric light was too dim.

He walked down the dark street a half block and then walked back and pressed the button beside the door; the door clicked open and he went through the short passageway into the long barroom.

A bartender wiped off the stained wood in front of him, questioned with his eyes.

Doolin said: "Rye."

He glanced idly at the men at the bar, at the tables, at the heavily built bald man who sat on a stool at the far end of the bar. The little bald man was stooped over a wide-spread newspaper.

The bartender put a glass on the bar in front of Doolin, put a flat brightly labeled flask beside it.

Doolin said: "Seen Martinelli tonight?"

The bartender watched Doolin pour his drink, picked up the bottle and put it under the bar, said: "Yeah. He came in a little while ago. He's upstairs."

Doolin nodded, tasted the rye. It wasn't too bad. He finished it and put a quarter on the bar, sauntered towards the door at the back of the room.

The little bald man looked up from his paper.

Doolin said: "Martinelli's expecting me. He's upstairs—ain't he?"

The little man looked at Doolin. He began at his face and went down to his feet and then back up, slowly. "He didn't say anything about you." He spat with the admirable precision of age and confidence into a cuspidor in the corner.

Doolin said: "He forgot." He put his hand on the doorknob.

The little man looked at him, through him, blankly.

Doolin turned the knob and opened the door, went through, closed the door behind him.

The stairs were dimly lighted by a sputtering gas-jet. He went up slowly. There was one door at the top of the first flight; it was dark; there was no light under it, no sound beyond it. Doolin went up another flight very quietly. He put his ear against the steel-sheathed door; he could hear no sound, but a little light filtered through under the door. He doubled up his fist, knocked with the heel of his hand.

Martinelli opened the door. He stood a moment staring questioningly at Doolin and then he glanced over his shoulder, smiled, said: "Come in."

Doolin put his hands in his overcoat pockets, his right hand holding the revolver tightly, went forward into the room.

Martinelli closed the door behind him, slid the heavy bolt.

The room was large, bare; somewhere around thirty-five by forty. It was lighted by a single green-shaded droplight over a very large round table in the center; there were other tables and chairs stacked in the dusk of the corner. There were no windows, no other doors.

Halloran sat in one of the four chairs at the table. He was leaning slightly forward with his elbows on the table, his long waxen hands framing his face. His face was entirely cold, white, expressionless.

Martinelli stood with his back against the door, his hands behind him.

Doolin glanced over his shoulder at Martinelli, looked back at Halloran. His eyebrows were lifted to the wide V, his mouth hung a little open.

Halloran said: "Well, well—this is a surprise."

He moved his eyes to Martinelli, said: "Angelo. Meet Mr Doolin—my bodyguard. . . ." For an instant his wide thin mouth flickered a fraction of an inch upward; then his face became a blank, white mask again. "Mr Doolin—Mr Martinelli. . . ."

Martinelli had silently come up behind Doolin, suddenly thrust his hands into Doolin's pockets, hard, grabbed Doolin's hands. Doolin bent sharply forward. They struggled for possibly half a minute, silently except for the tearing sound of their breath; then Martinelli brought his knee up suddenly, savagely; Doolin groaned, sank to his knees, the nickel-plated revolver clattered to the floor, slid halfway across the room.

Martinelli darted after it.

Halloran had not appeared to move. He said: "Wait a minute, baby. . . ." The blunt Luger that Doolin had experienced in the afternoon glittered on the table between his two hands.

Martinelli made an impatient gesture, stooped to pick up Doolin's gun.

"Wait a minute, baby." Halloran's voice was like a cold swift scythe.

Martinelli stood up very straight.

Doolin got to his feet slowly. He bent over and held the middle of his body, rolled his head toward Martinelli, his eyes narrow, malevolent. He said very quietly, as if to himself: "Dirty son of a bitch—dirty, *dirty* son of a bitch!"

Martinelli grinned, stood very straight. His hands, cupped close to his thighs, trembled rigidly.

Halloran said slowly: "Don't do it, baby. I'll shoot both your eyes out before you get that shiv of yours into the air—and never touch your nose."

Martinelli looked like a clothing store dummy. He was balanced on the balls of his feet, his hands trembling at his sides; his grin artificial, empty.

Doolin laughed suddenly. He stood up straight and looked at Martinelli and laughed.

Halloran moved his eyes to Doolin, smiled faintly.

He said: "Gentlemen—sit down."

Martinelli tottered forward, sank into one of the chairs.

Halloran said: "Put your hands on the table, please."

Martinelli obediently put his hands on the table. The empty grin seemed to have congealed on his face.

Halloran turned his eyes towards Doolin. Doolin smiled, walked gingerly to the other chair and sat down.

Halloran said: "Now. . . ." He put one hand up to his face; the other held the Luger loosely on the table.

Doolin cleared his throat, said: "What's it all about, Mr Halloran?"

Martinelli laughed suddenly. The empty grin exploded into loud high-pitched mirth. "What's it all about! Dear God—what's it all about! . . ."

Halloran was watching Doolin, his shadowed sunken eyes half closed.

Martinelli leaned forward, lifted his hands and pointed two fingers at Doolin. "Listen—wise guy. . . . You've got minutes to live—if you're lucky. That's what it's all about!"

Doolin regarded Martinelli with faint amusement.

Martinelli laughed again. He moved his hand slowly until the two fingers pointed at Halloran. "He killed Coleman," he said. "He shot Coleman an' I drove the car. An' he killed Winfield himself. An' his outfit killed Riccio an' Conroy. . . ."

Doolin glanced at Halloran, turned back to smile dimly, dumbly at Martinelli.

"He propositioned me into killing the dance-hall dame," Martinelli went on—"an' now he's going to kill you an' me. . . ."

Doolin grinned broadly but it was all done with his mouth. He didn't look like he felt it very much. He looked at Halloran. Halloran's face was white and immovable as plaster.

"Listen—wise-guy!" Martinelli leaned forward, moved his hand back to point at Doolin. He was suddenly very intense; his dark eyes burned into Doolin's. "I came out here for Riccio to make connections to peddle M——a lot of it—an' I met Mr Halloran." Martinelli moved his head an eighth of an inch towards Halloran. "Mr Halloran runs the drug racket out here—did you know that?"

Doolin glanced swiftly at Halloran, looked back at Martinelli's tense face.

"Mr Halloran aced me into double-crossing Frankie Riccio an' Conroy," Martinelli went on. "Mr Halloran's men rubbed Riccio an' Conroy, an' would've taken care of me if Riccio hadn't almost beat 'em to it. . . ."

Halloran said coldly, amusedly: "Oh—come, come, Angelo. . . ."

Martinelli did not look at Halloran. He said: "I met Riccio an' Conroy at the train that night an' took them to that joint in Culver City to talk business to Mr Halloran—only I didn't know the kind of business Mr Halloran was going to talk. . . ."

"Is it quite necessary to go into all this?" Halloran spoke sidewise to Martinelli, smiled at Doolin. It was his first definite change of expression since Doolin had come into the room.

Martinelli said: "Yes," emphatically. He scowled at Halloran, his eyes thin black slits. "Bright-boy here"—he indicated Doolin with his hand—"wants to know what it's all about. I'd like to have somebody know—besides me. One of us might leave here alive—if I get this all out of my system it's a cinch it won't be Bright-boy."

Halloran's smile was very cheerful. He said: "Go on."

"One of the men the Law picked up for the Hotspot shooting was a good guess—he's on Mr Halloran's payroll," Martinelli went on. He was accenting the "Mr" a little unnecessarily, a little too much. "When I got out of the hospital Mr Halloran suggested we clean things up—move Coleman an' Decker an' Winfield—anybody who might identify his man or testify that Riccio shot me—out of the way. He hated Winfield anyway, for beating his time with the Darmond gal—an' he hated her. . . ."

Halloran was beaming at Doolin, his hand tight and steady on the Luger. Doolin thought about the distance across the big table to Halloran, the distance to the light.

Martinelli was leaning forward, talking swiftly, eagerly: "I brought eighty-five grand worth of morphine out with me, an' I turned it over to his nibs here when we threw in together. I ain't had a nickel out of it. That's the reason I went for all this finagling—I wanted my dough. I was supposed to get it tonight, but I found out about ten minutes ago I ain't going to get it at all. . . ."

Martinelli smiled at Halloran, finished: "Mr Halloran says it was hi-jacked." He stood up slowly.

Halloran asked: "All through, baby?"

Martinelli was standing very stiff and straight, his hands cupped at his sides.

Doolin ducked suddenly, exerted all his strength to upset the table. For a moment he was protected by the edge, could see neither Martinelli nor Halloran; then the big round table-top slid off its metal base, crashed to the floor.

Halloran was holding Martinelli very much in the way a great ape would hold a smaller animal. One long arm was out stiff, the long white hand at Martinelli's throat, almost encircling it. Halloran's other hand held Martinelli's wrist, waved it back and forth slowly. The blade of a short curved knife glistened in Martinelli's hand. Except for the slow waving of their two hands they were as if frozen, entirely still. There was nothing human in their position, nothing human in their faces.

Doolin felt in that instant that Halloran was not human. He was mad, insane; but it was not the madness of a man, it was the cold murderous lust of an animal.

The Luger and Doolin's revolver were on the floor near their feet. Doolin circled until he was behind Halloran, moved slowly towards them.

As he dived for one of the guns Halloran swung Martinelli around swiftly, kicked viciously at Doolin's head. He missed once, but the second caught Doolin's hand as it closed over the Luger, sent the Luger spinning to a corner.

As Doolin half rose, Halloran's long leg lashed out again, his heavy shoe struck the side of Doolin's head. Doolin grunted, fell sidewise to the floor.

Doolin lay on his back and the room went around him. Later, in remembering what followed, it was like short strips of motion-picture film, separated by strips of darkness.

Halloran backed Martinelli slowly to the wall. It was as if they were performing some strange ritualistic dance; their steps were measured; Halloran's face was composed, his expression almost tender. Martinelli's face was darkening from the pressure on his throat. Halloran waved the hand holding the knife slowly back and forth.

The next time the darkness in Doolin's head cleared, they were against the wall, his head high, at a curious twisted angle above Halloran's white relentless hand, his face purpling. Halloran's other hand had slipped down over Martinelli's chest.

Martinelli's eyes bulged. His face was the face of a man who saw death coming, and was afraid. Doolin could no longer see Halloran's face. He watched the knife near Martinelli's chest, slowly.

Martinelli, some way, made a high piercing sound in his throat as the knife went into him. And again as Halloran withdrew the knife, pressed it in again slowly. Halloran did not stab mercifully on the left side, but on the right, puncturing the lung again and again, slowly.

Doolin rolled over on his side. The revolver lay on the floor midway between him and Halloran. He shook his head sharply, crawled towards it.

Halloran suddenly released Martinelli, stepped back a pace. Martinelli's knees buckled, he sank slowly down, sat on the floor with his back against the wall, his legs out straight. He sucked in air in great rattling gasps, held both hands tightly against his chest, tightly against the shaft of the knife.

He lifted his head and there was blood on his mouth. He laughed; and Doolin forgot the gun, stopped, stared fascinated at Martinelli. Martinelli laughed and the sound was as if everything inside him was breaking. His head rolled back and he grinned upward with glazing eyes at Halloran, held his hands tightly against his chest, spoke:

"Tell Lola we can't go away now. . . ." He paused, sucked in air. "She's waiting for me. . . . Tell her Angelo sends his regrets. . . ." His voice was thick, high-pitched, but his words were telling, deadly, took deadly effect.

Halloran seemed to grow taller, his great shoulders seemed to widen as Doolin watched.

Martinelli laughed again. He said: "So long— sucker. . . ."

Halloran kicked him savagely in the chest. He drew his

long leg back and as Martinelli slumped sidewise he kicked his face, hard, repeatedly.

Doolin scrambled swiftly forward, picked up the revolver, raised it.

Halloran turned slowly.

Doolin held the revolver unsteadily in his right hand, aimed at Halloran's chest while the muzzle described little circles, pulled the trigger twice.

Halloran came towards him. Doolin made a harsh sound in his throat, scuttled backwards a few feet, held the revolver out limply and fired again.

Halloran's face was cold, impassive; his eyes were great black holes in his skull. He came towards Doolin slowly.

Doolin tried to say something but the words stuck in his throat, and then Halloran was above him and there was a terribly crushing weight against Doolin's forehead and it was suddenly dark.

Slowly, Doolin came to, lay a little while with his eyes closed. There were sharp twisting wires of pain in his head; he put his hand up, took it away wet, sticky.

He opened his eyes. It was entirely dark, a cold penetrating darkness; entirely still.

Suddenly he laughed, a curious hysterical sound in the quiet room; and as suddenly, panic seized him. He struggled to his knees, almost fell down again as the pain in his head throbbed to the swift movement. He got to his feet slowly, fumbled in his pockets and found a match, lighted it.

Martinelli's body was slumped in the angle of floor and wall at one side of the room. There was no one else. Doolin's revolver shone dimly on the floor in the flare of the match. The door was ajar.

Doolin lighted another match and picked up his revolver, his hat. He took out a handkerchief and wiped his face and the handkerchief was wet, dark. He walked, unsteadily to the door, down the dark stairs.

One faint globe burned above the deserted bar. Doolin felt his way along the wall, lifted the heavy bar across the outside door and went out, closed the door behind him. It was raining lightly, a thin cold drizzle.

He took air into his lungs in great gulps, soaked the handkerchief in a little puddle of rainwater and tried to clean his face. Then he went down the dark street swiftly towards Broadway.

The druggist looked at him through thick spectacles, gestured towards the back of the store.

Doolin said: "Fix me up some peroxide an' bandages an' stuff—I had an accident." He went back to the telephone booth, found the number of the Fontenoy, called it, asked for Mrs Sare.

The operator said Mrs Sare didn't answer.

Doolin hung up and went out and cleaned the blood from his face in front of a mirror. A little girl stared at him wide-eyed from the soda fountain; the druggist said: "Automobile . . . ?"

Doolin nodded.

The druggist asked: "How much bandage do you want?"

Doolin said: "Let it go—it's not as bad as I thought it was."

He put his hat on the back of his head and went out and got into a cab, said: "Fontenoy Apartments—Hollywood. An' make it snappy."

Lola Sare's voice said: "Yes," with rising inflection.

Doolin opened the door, went in.

She was sitting in a long low chair beneath a crimson-shaded bridge lamp. It was the only light in the room. Her arms were bare, straight on the arms of the chair, her hands hanging limply downward. Her dark head was against the back of the chair and her face was taut, her eyes wide, vacant.

Doolin took off his hat, said: "Why the hell don't you answer your phone?"

She did not speak, nor move.

"You'd better get out of here—quick." Doolin went towards her. "Halloran killed Martinelli—an' Martinelli opened up about you before he died. Halloran will be coming to see you. . . ."

Her blank eyes moved slowly from his face to some place in the dusk behind him. He followed her gaze, turned slowly.

Halloran was standing against the wall near the door. The door had covered him when Doolin entered; he put out one

93

hand and pushed it gently, it swung closed with a sharp click.

As Doolin's eyes became used to the dimness of the room he saw Halloran clearly. He was leaning against the wall and the right shoulder and breast of his light gray suit was dark, sodden. He held the short blunt Luger in his left hand.

He said: "You're a little late. . . ."

The Luger roared.

Lola Sare put her hands up to the middle of her breast, low; her head came forward slowly. She started to get up and the Luger leaped in Halloran's hand, roared again.

At the same instant Doolin shot, holding the revolver low. The two explosions were simultaneous, thundered in the dark and narrow room.

Halloran fell as a tree falls; slowly, stiffly, his arm stiff at his sides; crashed to the floor.

Doolin dropped the revolver, walked unsteadily towards Lola Sare. His knees buckled suddenly and he sank forward, down.

There was someone pounding at the door

Doolin finished dabbing iodine on his head, washed his hands and went into the little living room of his apartment. A first dull streak of morning grayed the windows. He pulled down the shades and went into the kitchenette, lighted the gas under the percolator.

When the coffee was hot he poured a cup, dropped four lumps of sugar into it absently, carried it into the living room. He sat down on the davenport and put the coffee on an endtable, picked up the phone and dialed a number.

He said: "Hello, Grace? Is Mollie there? . . ." He listened a moment, went on: "Oh—I thought she might be there. Sorry I woke you up. . . ." He hung up, sipped his steaming coffee.

After a few minutes he picked up the phone, dialed again, said. "Listen, Grace—please put Mollie on. . . . Aw nuts! I know she's there—please make her talk to me. . . ."

Then he smiled, waited a moment, said: "Hello darling . . . Listen—please come on home—will you? . . . Aw listen, Honey—I did what you said—everything's all right. . . . Uh-huh. . . . Halloran's dead—an' Martinelli

94

. . . . Uh-huh. . . . The Sare dame is shot up pretty bad, but not too much to give evidence an' clean it all up. . . . Uh-huh. . . ."

He reached over and picked up the cup and took a long drink of coffee, smiled into the phone, said: "Sure—I'm all right—I got a little scratch on my head but I'm all right. . . . Sure. . . . Sure—we were right. . . . All right, Honey—I'll be waiting for you. Hurry up. . . . G'bye. . . ."

He hung up, curved his mouth to a wide grin, finished his coffee, lit a cigarette and waited.

PIGEON BLOOD

The woman was bent far forward over the steering-wheel of the open roadster. Her eyes, narrowed to long black-fringed slits, moved regularly down and up, from the glistening road ahead, to the small rear-view mirror above the windshield. The two circles of white light in the mirror grew steadily larger. She pressed the throttle slowly, steadily downward; there was no sound but the roar of the wind and the deep purr of the powerful engine.

There was a sudden sharp crack; a little frosted circle appeared on the windshield. The woman pressed the throttle to the floor. She was pale; her eyes were suddenly large and dark and afraid, her lips were pressed tightly together. The tires screeched on the wet pavement as the car roared around a long, shallow curve. The headlights of the pursuing car grew larger.

The second and third shots were wild, or buried themselves harmlessly in the body of the car; the fourth struck the left rear tire and the car swerved crazily, skidded halfway across the road. Very suddenly there was bright yellow light right ahead, at the side of the road. The woman jammed on the brakes, jerked the wheel hard over; the tires slid, screamed raggedly over the gravel in front of the gas station, the car stopped. The other car went by at seventy-five miles an hour. One last shot thudded into the back of the seat beside the woman and then the other car had disappeared into the darkness.

Two men ran out of the gas station. Another man stood in the doorway. The woman was leaning back straight in the seat and her eyes were very wide; she was breathing hard, unevenly.

One of the men put his hand on her shoulder, asked: "Are you all right, lady?"

She nodded.

97

The other man asked: "Hold-ups?" He was a short, middle-aged man and his eyes were bright, interested.

The woman opened her bag and took out a cigarette. She said shakily: "I guess so." She pulled out the dashboard lighter, waited until it glowed red and held it to her cigarette.

The younger man was inspecting the back of the car. He said: "They punctured the tank. It's a good thing you stopped—you couldn't have gone much farther."

"Yes—I guess it's a very good thing I stopped," she said, mechanically. She took a deep drag of her cigarette.

The other man said: "That's the third hold-up out here this week."

The woman spoke to the younger man. "Can you get me a cab?"

He said: "Sure." Then he knelt beside the blown-out tire, said: "Look, Ed—they almost cut it in two."

The man in the doorway called to her: "You want a cab, lady?"

She smiled, nodded, and the man disappeared into the gas station; he came back to the doorway in a minute, over to the car. "There'll be a cab here in a little while, lady," he said.

She thanked him.

"This is one of the worst stretches of road on Long Island—for highwaymen." He leaned on the door of the car. "Did they try to nudge you off the road—or did they just start shooting?"

"They just started shooting."

He said: "We got a repair service here—do you want us to fix up your car?"

She nodded. "How long will it take?"

"Couple days. We'll have to get a new windshield from the branch factory in Queens—an' take off that tank. . . ."

She took a card out of her bag and gave it to him, said: "Call me up when it's finished."

After a little while, a cab came out of the darkness of a side street, turned into the station. The woman got out of the car and went over to the cab, spoke to the driver: "Do you know any shortcuts into Manhattan? Somebody tried to hold me up on the main road a little while ago, and maybe they're still laying for me. I don't want any more of it—I want to go home." She was very emphatic.

The driver was a big red-faced Irishman. He grinned, said: "Lady—I know a million of 'em. You'll be as safe with me as you'd be in your own home."

She raised her hand in a gesture of farewell to the three men around her car and got into the cab. After the cab had disappeared, the man to whom she had given the card took it out of his pocket and squinted at it, read aloud: "Mrs Dale Hanan—Five-eighty Park Avenue."

The short, middle-aged man bobbed his head knowingly. "Sure," he said—"I knew she was class. She's Hanan's wife—the millionaire. Made his dough in oil—Oklahoma. His chauffeur told me how he got his start—didn't have a shoestring or a place to put it, so he shot off his big toe and collected ten grand on an accident policy—grubstake on his first well. Bright boy. He's got a big estate down at Roslyn."

The man with the card nodded. He said: "That's swell. We can soak him plenty." He put the card back into his pocket.

When the cab stopped near the corner of Sixty-third and Park Avenue the woman got out, paid the driver and hurried into the apartment house. In her apartment, she put in a long-distance call to Roslyn, Long Island; when the connection had been made, she said: "Dale—it's in the open, now. I was followed, driving back to town—shot at—the car was nearly wrecked. . . . I don't know what to do. Even if I call Crandall, now, and tell him I won't go through with it—won't go to the police—he'll probably have me killed, just to make sure. . . . Yes, I'm going to stay in—I'm scared. . . . All right, dear. 'Bye."

She hung up, went to a wide center table and poured whiskey into a tall glass, sat down and stared vacantly at the glass—her hand was shaking a little. She smiled suddenly, crookedly, lifted the glass to her mouth and drained it. Then she put the glass on the floor and leaned back and glanced at the tiny watch at her wrist. It was ten minutes after nine.

At a few minutes after ten a black Packard town-car stopped in front of a narrow building of gray stone on East

Fifty-fourth Street; a tall man got out, crossed the sidewalk and rang the bell. The car went on. When the door swung open, the tall man went into a long, brightly lighted hallway, gave his hat and stick to the checkroom attendant, went swiftly up two flights of narrow stairs to the third floor. He glanced around the big, crowded room, then crossed to one corner near a window on the Fifty-fourth Street side and sat down at a small table, smiled wanly at the man across from him, said: "Mister Druse, I believe."

The other man was about fifty, well set up, well-groomed in the way of good living. His thick gray hair was combed sharply, evenly back. He lowered his folded newspaper to the table, stared thoughtfully at the tall man.

He said: "Mister Hanan," and his voice was very deep, metallic.

The tall man nodded shortly, leaned back and folded his arms across his narrow chest. He was ageless, perhaps thirty-five, forty-five; his thin, colorless hair was close-clipped, his long, bony face deeply tanned, a sharp and angular setting for large seal-brown eyes. His mouth was curved, mobile.

He asked: "Do you know Jeffrey Crandall?"

Druse regarded him evenly, expressionlessly for a moment, raised his head and beckoned a waiter. Hanan ordered a whiskey sour.

Druse said: "I know Mister Crandall casually. Why?"

"A little more than an hour ago Crandall, or Crandall's men, tried to murder Mrs Hanan, as she was driving back from my place at Roslyn." Hanan leaned forward: his eyes were wide, worried.

The waiter served Hanan's whiskey sour, set a small bottle of Perrier and a small glass on the table in front of Druse.

Druse poured the water into the glass slowly. "So what?"

Hanan tasted his drink. He said: "This is not a matter for the police, Mister Druse. I understand that you interest yourself in things of this nature, so I took the liberty of calling you and making this appointment. Is that right?" He was nervous, obviously ill at ease.

Druse shrugged. "*What* nature? I don't know what you're talking about."

"I'm sorry—I guess I'm a little upset." Hanan smiled.

100

"What I mean is that I can rely on your discretion?"

Druse frowned. "I think so," he said slowly. He drank half of the Perrier, squinted down at the glass as if it tasted very badly.

Hanan smiled vacantly. "You do not know Mrs Hanan?"

Druse shook his head slowly, turned his glass around and around on the table.

"We have been living apart for several years," Hanan went on. "We are still very fond of one another, we are very good friends, but we do not get along—together. Do you understand?"

Druse nodded.

Hanan sipped his drink, went on swiftly: "Catherine has—has always had—a decided weakness for gambling. She went through most of her own inheritance—a considerable inheritance—before we were married. Since our separation she has lost somewhere in the neighborhood of a hundred and fifteen thousand dollars. I have, of course, taken care of her debts." Hanan coughed slightly. "Early this evening she called me at Roslyn, said she had to see me immediately—that it was very important. I offered to come into town but she said she'd rather come out. She came out about seven."

Hanan paused, closed his eyes and rubbed two fingers of one hand slowly up and down his forehead. "She's in a very bad jam with Crandall." He opened his eyes and put his hand down on the table.

Druse finished his Perrier, put down the glass and regarded Hanan attentively.

"About three weeks ago," Hanan went on, "Catherine's debt to Crandall amounted to sixty-eight thousand dollars—she had been playing very heavily under the usual gambler's delusion of getting even. She was afraid to come to me—she knew I'd taken several bad beatings on the market—she kept putting it off and trying to make good her losses, until Crandall demanded the money. She told him she couldn't pay—together, they hatched out a scheme to get it. Catherine had a set of rubies—pigeon blood—been in her family five or six generations. They're worth, perhaps, a hundred and seventy-five thousand—her father insured them for a hundred and thirty-five, forty years ago and the

101

insurance premiums have always been paid. . . ." Hanan finished his whiskey sour, leaned back in his chair.

Druse said: "I assume the idea was that the rubies disappear; that Mrs Hanan claim the insurance, pay off Crandall, have sixty-seven thousand left and live happily forever after."

Hanan coughed; his face was faintly flushed. "Exactly."

"I assume further," Druse went on, "that the insurance company did not question the integrity of the claim; that they paid, and that Mrs Hanan, in turn, paid Crandall."

Hanan nodded. He took a tortoise-shell case out of his pocket, offered Druse a cigarette.

Druse shook his head, asked: "Are the insurance company detectives warm—are they making Crandall or whoever he had do the actual job, uncomfortable?"

"No. The theft was well engineered. I don't think Crandall is worrying about that." Hanan lighted a cigarette. "But Catherine wanted her rubies back—as had, of course, been agreed upon." He leaned forward, put his elbows on the table. "Crandall returned paste imitations to her—she only discovered they weren't genuine a few days ago."

Druse smiled, said slowly: "In that case, I should think it was Crandall who was in a jam with Mrs Hanan, instead of Mrs Hanan who was in a jam with Crandall."

Hanan wagged his long chin back and forth. "This is New York. Men like Crandall do as they please. Catherine went to him and he laughed at her; said the rubies he had returned were the rubies that had been stolen. She had no recourse, other than to admit her complicity in defrauding the insurance company. That's the trouble—she threatened to do exactly that."

Druse widened his eyes, stared at Hanan.

"Catherine is a very impulsive woman," Hanan went on. "She was so angry at losing the rubies and being made so completely a fool, that she threatened Crandall. She told him that if the rubies were not returned within three days she would tell what he had done; that he had stolen the rubies—take her chances on her part in it coming out. Of course she wouldn't do it, but she was desperate and she thought that was her only chance of scaring Crandall into returning the rubies—and she made him believe it. Since

102

she talked to him, Wednesday, she has been followed. Tomorrow is Saturday, the third day. Tonight, driving back to town, she was followed, shot at—almost killed."

"Has she tried to get in touch with Crandall again?"

Hanan shook his head. "She's been stubbornly waiting for him to give the rubies back—until this business tonight. Now she's frightened—says it wouldn't do any good for her to talk to Crandall now because he wouldn't believe her—and it's too easy for him to put her out of the way."

Druse beckoned the waiter, asked him to bring the check. "Where is she now?"

"At her apartment—Sixty-third and Park."

"What do you intend doing about it?"

Hanan shrugged. "That's what I came to you for. I don't know what to do. I've heard of you and your work from friends. . . ."

Druse hesitated, said slowly: "I must make my position clear."

Hanan nodded, lighted a fresh cigarette.

"I am one of the few people left," Druse went on, "who actually believes that honesty is the best policy. Honesty is my business—I am primarily a business man—I've made it pay."

Hanan smiled broadly.

Druse leaned forward. "I am not a fixer," he said. "My acquaintance is wide and varied—I am fortunate in being able to wield certain influences. But above all I seek to further justice—I mean real justice as opposed to *book* justice—I was on the Bench for many years and I realize the distinction keenly." His big face wrinkled to an expansive grin. "And I get paid for it—*well* paid."

Hanan said: "Does my case interest you?"

"It does."

"Will five thousand be satisfactory—as a retaining fee?"

Druse moved his broad shoulders in something like a shrug. "You value the rubies at a hundred and seventy-five thousand," he said. "I am undertaking to get the rubies back, and protect Mrs Hanan's life." He stared at Hanan intently. "What value do you put on Mrs Hanan's life?"

Hanan frowned self-consciously, twisted his mouth down at the corners. "That is, of course, impossible to—"

"Say another hundred and seventy-five." Druse smiled easily. "That makes three hundred and fifty thousand. I work on a ten per cent basis—thirty-five thousand—one-third in advance." He leaned back, still smiling easily. "Ten thousand will be sufficient as a retainer."

Hanan was still frowning self-consciously. He said: "Done," took a checkbook and fountain pen out of his pocket.

Druse went on: "If I fail in either purpose, I shall, of course, return your check."

Hanan bobbed his head, made out the check in a minute, illegible scrawl and handed it across the table. Druse paid for the drinks, jotted down Hanan's telephone number and the address of Mrs Hanan's apartment. They got up and went downstairs and out of the place; Druse told Hanan he would call him within an hour, got into a cab. Hanan watched the cab disappear in east-bound traffic, lighted a cigarette nervously and walked towards Madison Avenue.

Druse said: "Tell her I've come from Mister Hanan."

The telephone operator spoke into the transmitter, turned to Druse. "You may go up—Apartment Three D."

When, in answer to a drawled, "Come in," he pushed open the door and went into the apartment, Catherine Hanan was standing near the center table, with one hand on the table to steady herself, the other in the pocket of her long blue robe. She was beautiful in the mature way that women who have lived too hard, too swiftly, are sometimes beautiful. She was very dark; her eyes were large, liquid, black and dominated her rather small, sharply sculptured face. Her mouth was large, deeply red, not particularly strong.

Druse bowed slightly, said: "How do you do."

She smiled, and her eyes were heavy, nearly closed. "Swell—and you?"

He came slowly into the room, put his hat on the table, asked: "May we sit down?"

"Sure." She jerked her head towards a chair, stayed where she was.

Druse said: "You're drunk."

"Right."

104

He smiled, sighed gently. "A commendable condition. I regret exceedingly that my stomach does not permit it." He glanced casually about the room. In the comparative darkness of a corner, near a heavily draped window, there was a man lying on his back on the floor. His arms were stretched out and back, and his legs were bent under him in a curious broken way, and there was blood on his face.

Druse raised his thick white eyebrows, spoke without looking at Mrs Hanan: "Is *he* drunk, too?"

She laughed shortly. "Uh-huh—in a different way." She nodded towards a golf-stick on the floor near the man. "He had a little too much niblick."

"Friend of yours?"

She said: "I rather doubt it. He came in from the fire-escape with a gun in his hand. I happened to see him before he saw me."

"Where's the gun?"

"I've got it." She drew a small black automatic half out of the pocket of her robe.

Druse went over and knelt beside the man, picked up one of his hands. He said slowly: "This man is decidedly dead."

Mrs Hanan stood, staring silently at the man on the floor for perhaps thirty seconds. Her face was white, blank. Then she walked unsteadily to a desk against one wall and picked up a whiskey bottle, poured a stiff drink. She said: "I know it." Her voice was choked, almost a whisper. She drank the whiskey, turned and leaned against the desk, stared at Druse with wide unseeing eyes. "So what?"

"So pull yourself together, and forget about it—we've got more important things to think about for a little while." Druse stood up. "How long ago? . . ."

She shuddered. "About a half-hour—I didn't know what to do. . . ."

"Have you tried to reach Crandall? I mean before this happened—right after you came in tonight?"

"Yes—I couldn't get him."

Druse went to a chair and sat down. He said: "Mister Hanan has turned this case over to me. Won't you sit down, and answer a few questions? . . ."

She sank into a low chair near the desk. "Are you a detective?" Her voice was still very low, strained.

105

Druse smiled. "I'm an attorney—a sort of extra-legal attorney." He regarded her thoughtfully. "If we can get your rubies back, and assure your safety, and"—he coughed slightly—"induce Mister Hanan to reimburse the insurance company, you will be entirely satisfied, will you not?"

She nodded, started to speak.

Druse interrupted her: "Are the rubies themselves—I mean intrinsically, as stones—awfully important to you? Or was this grandstand play of yours—this business of threatening Crandall—motivated by rather less tangible factors—such as self-respect, things like that?"

She smiled faintly, nodded. "God knows how I happen to have any self-respect left—I've been an awful ass—but I have. It was the idea of being made such a fool—after I've lost over a hundred thousand dollars to Crandall—that made me do it."

Druse smiled. "The rubies themselves," he said—"I mean the rubies as stones—entirely apart from any extraneous consideration such as self-respect—would more seriously concern Mister Hanan, would they not?"

She said: "Sure. He's always been crazy about stones."

Druse scratched the tip of his long nose pensively. His eyes were wide and vacant, his thick lips compressed to a long downward curved line. "You are sure you were followed when you left Crandall's Wednesday?"

"As sure as one can be without actually knowing—it was more of a followed feeling than anything else. After the idea was planted I could have sworn I saw a dozen men, of course."

He said: "Have you ever had that feeling before—I mean before you threatened Crandall?"

"No."

"It may have been simply imagination, because you expected to be followed—there was reason for you to be followed?"

She nodded. "But it's a cinch it wasn't imagination this evening."

Druse was leaning forward, his elbows on his knees. He looked intently at her, said very seriously: "I'm going to get your rubies back, and I can assure you of your safety—and I think I can promise that the matter of reimbursement to the insurance company will be taken care of. I didn't speak to Mister Hanan about that, but I'm sure he'll see the justice of it."

She smiled faintly.

Druse went on: "I promise you these things—and in return I want you to do exactly as I tell you until tomorrow morning."

Her smile melted to a quick, rather drunken, laugh. "Do I have to poison any babies?" She stood up, poured a drink.

Druse said: "*That's* one of the things I *don't* want you to do."

She picked up the glass, frowned at him with mock seriousness. "You're a moralist," she said. "That's one of the things I *will* do."

He shrugged slightly. "I shall have some very important, very delicate work for you a little later in the evening. I thought it might be best."

She looked at him, half smiling, a little while, and then she laughed and put down the glass and went into the bathroom. He leaned back comfortably in the chair and stared at the ceiling; his hands were on the arms of the chair and he ran imaginary scales with his big blunt fingers.

She came back into the room in a little while, dressed, drawing on gloves. She gestured with her head towards the man on the floor, and for a moment her more or less alcoholic poise forsook her—she shuddered again—her face was white, twisted.

Druse stood up, said: "He'll have to stay where he is for a little while." He went to the heavily draped window, to the fire-escape, moved the drape aside and locked the window. "How many doors are there to the apartment?"

"Two." She was standing near the table. She took the black automatic from a pocket of her suit, took up a gray suede bag from the table and put the automatic into it.

He watched her without expression. "How many keys?"

"Two." She smiled, took two keys out of the bag and held them up. "The only other key is the pass-key—the manager's."

He said: "That's fine," went to the table and picked up his hat and put it on. They went out into the hall and closed and

107

locked the door. "Is there a side entrance to the building?"

She nodded.

"Let's go out that way."

She led the way down the corridor, down three flights of stairs to a door leading to Sixty-third Street. They went out and walked over Sixty-third to Lexington and got into a cab; he told the driver to take them to the corner of Fortieth and Madison, leaned back and looked out the window. "How long have you and Mister Hanan been divorced?"

She was quick to answer: "Did he say we were divorced?"

"No." Druse turned to her slowly, smiled slowly.

"Then what makes you think we are?"

"I don't. I just wanted to be sure."

"We are *not*." She was very emphatic.

He waited, without speaking.

She glanced at him sidewise and saw that he expected her to go on. She laughed softly. "He wants a divorce. He asked me to divorce him several months ago." She sighed, moved her hands nervously on her lap. "That's another of the things I'm not very proud of—I wouldn't do it. I don't quite know why—we were never in love—we haven't been married, really, for a long time—but I've waited, hoping we might be able to make something out of it. . . ."

Druse said quietly: "I think I understand—I'm sorry I had to ask you about that."

She did not answer.

In a little while the cab stopped; they got out and Druse paid the driver and they cut diagonally across the street, entered an office building halfway down the block. Druse spoke familiarly to the Negro elevator boy; they got off at the forty-fifth floor and went up two flights of narrow stairs, through a heavy steel fire-door to a narrow bridge and across it to a rambling two-story penthouse that covered all one side of the roof. Druse rang the bell and a thin-faced Filipino boy let them in.

Druse led the way into a very big, high-ceilinged room that ran the length and almost the width of the house. It was beautifully and brightly furnished, opened on one side onto a wide terrace. They went through to the terrace; there were steamer-chairs there and canvas swings and low round tables, a great many potted plants and small trees. The tiled floor was partially covered with strips of coco-matting. There was a very wide, vividly striped awning stretched across all one side. At the far side, where the light from the living room faded into darkness, the floor came to an abrupt end—there was no railing or parapet—the nearest building of the same height was several blocks away.

Mrs Hanan sat down and stared at the twinkling distant lights of Upper Manhattan. The roar of the city came up to them faintly, like surf very far away. She said: "It is very beautiful."

"I am glad you find it so." Druse went to the edge, glanced down. "I have never put a railing here," he said, "because I am interested in Death. Whenever I'm depressed I look at my jumping-off place, only a few feet away, and am reminded that life is very sweet." He stared at the edge, stroked the side of his jaw with his fingers. "Nothing to climb over, no windows to raise—just walk."

She smiled wryly. "A moralist—and morbid. Did you bring me here to suggest a suicide pact?"

"I brought you here to sit still and be decorative."

"And you?"

"I'm going hunting." Druse went over and stood frowning down at her. "I'll try not to be long. The boy will bring you anything you want—even *good* whiskey, if you can't get along without it. The view will grow on you—you'll find one of the finest collections of books on satanism, demonol-ogy, witchcraft, in the world inside." He gestured with his head and eyes. "Don't telephone anyone—and, above all, *stay* here, even if I'm late."

She nodded vaguely.

He went to the wide doors that led into the living room, turned, said: "One thing more—who are Mister Hanan's attorneys?"

She looked at him curiously. "Mahlon and Stiles."

He raised one hand in salute. "So long."

She smiled, said: "So long—good hunting."

He went into the living room and talked to the Filipino boy a minute, went out.

In the drugstore across the street from the entrance to the building, he went into a telephone booth, called the number Hanan had given him. When Hanan answered, he said: "I have very bad news. We were too late. When I reached Mrs Hanan's apartment, she did not answer the phone—I bribed my way in and found her—found her dead. . . . I'm terribly sorry, old man—you've got to take it standing up. . . . Yes—strangled."

Druse smiled grimly to himself. "No, I haven't informed the police—I want things left as they are for the present— I'm going to see Crandall and I have a way of working it so he won't have a single out. I'm going to pin it on him so that it will stay pinned—and I'm going to get the rubies back, too. . . . I know they don't mean much to you now, but the least I can do is get them back—and see that Crandall is stuck so he can't wriggle out of it." He said the last very emphatically, was silent a little while, except for an occasionally interjected "Yes" or "No."

Finally he asked: "Can you be in around three-thirty or four? . . . I'll want to get in touch with you then. . . . Right, I know how you must feel—I'm terribly sorry. . . . Right. Good-bye." He hung up and went out into Fortieth Street.

Jeffrey Crandall was a medium-sized man with a close-cropped mustache, wide-set greenish gray eyes. He was conservatively dressed, looked very much like a prosperous real estate man, or broker.

He said: "Long time no see."

Druse nodded abstractedly. He was sitting in a deep red leather chair in Crandall's very modern office, adjoining the large room in a midtown apartment building that was Crandall's "Place" for the moment. He raised his head and looked attentively at the pictures on the walls, one after the other.

"Anything special?" Crandall lighted a short stub of green cigar.

Druse said: "Very special," over his shoulder. He came to the last picture, a very ordinary Degas pastel, shook his head slightly, disapprovingly, and turned back to Crandall. He took a short-barrelled derringer out of his inside coat-pocket, held it on the arm of his chair, the muzzle focused steadily on Crandall's chest.

Crandall's eyes widened slowly; his mouth hung a little

open. He put one hand up very slowly and took the stub of a cigar out of his mouth.

Druse repeated: "Very special." His full lips were curved to a thin, cold smile.

Crandall stared at the gun. He spoke as if making a tremendous effort to frame his words casually, calmly: "What's it all about?"

"It's all about Mrs Hanan." Druse tipped his hat to the back of his head. "It's all about you gypping her out of her rubies—and her threatening to take it to the police—and you having her murdered at about a quarter after ten tonight, because you were afraid she'd go through with it."

Crandall's tense face relaxed slowly; he tried very hard to smile. He said: "You're crazy," and there was fear in his eyes, fear in the harsh, hollow sound of his voice.

Druse did not speak. He waited, his cold eyes boring into Crandall's.

Crandall cleared his throat, moved a little forward in his chair and put his elbows on the wide desk.

"Don't ring." Druse glanced at the little row of ivory push buttons on the desk, shook his head.

Crandall laughed soundlessly as if the thought of ringing had never entered his mind. "In the first place," he said, "I gave her back the stones that were stolen. In the second place, I never believed her gag about telling about it." He leaned back slowly, spoke very slowly and distinctly as confidence came back to him. "In the third place, I couldn't be chump enough to bump her off with that kind of a case against me."

Druse said: "Your third place is the one that interests me. The switched rubies, her threat to tell the story—it all makes a pip of a case against you, doesn't it?"

Crandall nodded slowly.

"That's the reason," Druse went on, "that if I shoot you through the heart right now, I'll get a vote of thanks for avenging the lady you made a sucker of, and finally murdered because you thought she was going to squawk."

All the fear came back into Crandall's face suddenly. He started to speak.

Druse interrupted him, went on: "I'm going to let you have it when you reach for your gun, of course—that'll take

111

care of any technicalities about taking the law into my own hands—anything like that."

Crandall's face was white, drained. He said: "How come I'm elected? What the hell have you got against me?"

Druse shrugged. "You shouldn't jockey ladies into trying to nick insurance companies. . . ."

"It was her idea."

"Then you should have been on the level about the rubies."

Crandall said: "So help me God! I gave her back the stuff I took!" He said it very vehemently, very earnestly.

"How do you know? How do you know the man you had do the actual job didn't make the switch?"

Crandall leaned forward. "Because *I* took them. She gave me her key and I went in the side way, while she was out, and took them myself. They were never out of my hands." He took up a lighter from the desk and relighted the stump of cigar with shaking hands. "That's the reason I didn't take her threat seriously. I thought it was some kind of extortion gag she'd doped out to get some of her dough back. She got back the stones I took—and if they weren't genuine they were switched before I took them, or after I gave them back."

Druse stared at him silently for perhaps a minute, finally smiled, said: "Before."

Crandall sucked noisily at his cigar. "Then, if you believe me"—he glanced at the derringer—"what's the point?"

"The point is that if I didn't believe you, you'd be in an awfully bad spot."

Crandall nodded, grinned weakly.

"The point," Druse went on, "is that you're still in an awfully bad spot because no one else will believe you."

Crandall nodded again. He leaned back and took a handkerchief out of his breast pocket and dabbed at his face.

"I know a way out of it." Druse moved his hand, let the derringer hang by the trigger-guard from his forefinger. "Not because I like you particularly, nor because I think you particularly deserve it—but because it's right. I can turn up the man who really murdered her—if we can get back the rubies—the real rubies. And I think I know where they are."

112

Crandall was leaning far forward, his face very alive and interested.

"I want you to locate the best peterman we can get." Druse spoke in a very low voice, watched Crandall intently. "We've got to open a safe—I think it'll be a safe—out on Long Island. Nothing very difficult—there'll probably be servants to handle but nothing more serious than that."

Crandall said: "Why can't I do it?" He smiled a little. "I used to be in the box business, you know—before I straightened up and got myself a joint. That's the reason I took the fake rubies myself—not to let anyone else in on it."

Druse said: "That'll be fine."

"When?" Crandall stood up.

Druse put the derringer back in his pocket. "Right now—where's your car?"

Crandall jerked his head towards the street. They went out through the crowded gambling room, downstairs, got into Crandall's car. Crossing Queensborough Bridge Druse glanced at his watch. It was twenty minutes past twelve.

At three thirty-five Druse pushed the bell of the penthouse, after searching, vainly as usual, for his key. The Filipino boy opened the door, said: "It's a very hot night, sir."

Druse threw his hat on a chair, smiled sadly at Mrs Hanan, who had come into the little entrance-hall. "I've been trying to teach him English for three months," he said, "and all he can say is 'Yes sir,' and 'No, sir,' and tell me about the heat." He turned to the broadly grinning boy. "Yes, Tony, it is a very hot night."

They went through the living room, out onto the terrace. It was cool there, and dim; a little light came out through the wide doors, from the living room.

Mrs Hanan said: "I'd about given you up."

Druse sat down, sighed wearily. "I've had a very strenuous evening—sorry I'm so late." He looked up at her. "Hungry?"

"Starved."

"Why didn't you have Tony fix you something?"

"I wanted to wait." She had taken off her suit-coat, hat; in her smartly cut tweed skirt, white mannish shirt, she looked very beautiful.

Druse said: "Supper, or breakfast, or something will be

113

ready in a few minutes—I ordered it for four." He stood up. "Which reminds me—we're having a guest. I must telephone."

He went through the living room, up four broad, shallow steps to the little corner room that he used as an office. He sat down at the broad desk, drew the telephone towards him, dialed a number.

Hanan answered the phone. Druse said: "I want you to come to my place, on top of the Pell Building, at once. It is very important. Ring the bell downstairs—I've told the elevator boy I'm expecting you. . . . I can't tell you over the phone—please come alone, and right away." He hung up and sat staring vacantly at his hands a little while, and then got up and went back to the terrace, sat down.

"What did you do with yourself?"

Mrs Hanan was lying in one of the low chairs. She laughed nervously. "The radio—tried to improve my Spanish and Tony's English—chewed my fingernails—almost frightened myself to death with one of your damned demon books." She lighted a cigarette. "And you?"

He smiled in the darkness. "I earned thirty-five thousand dollars."

She sat up, said eagerly: "Did you get the rubies?"

He nodded.

"Did Crandall raise much hell?"

"Enough."

She laughed exultantly. "Where are they?"

Druse tapped his pocket, watched her face in the pale orange glow of her cigarette.

She got up, held out her hand. "May I see them?"

Druse said: "Certainly." He took a long flat jewel-case of black velvet out of his inside coat-pocket and handed it to her.

She opened the case and went to the door to the living room, looked at its contents by the light there, said: "They are awfully beautiful, aren't they?"

"They are."

She snapped the case closed, came back and sat down.

Druse said: "I think I'd better take care of them a little while longer."

She leaned forward and put the case on his lap; he took it

114

up and put it back in his pocket. They sat silently, watching the lights in buildings over towards the East River. After awhile the Filipino boy came out and said that they were served.

"Our guest is late." Druse stood up. "I make a rule of never waiting breakfast—anything but breakfast."

They went together through the living room, into the simply furnished dining room. There were three places set at the glittering white and silver table. They sat down and the Filipino boy brought in tall and spindly cocktail glasses of iced fruit; they were just beginning when the doorbell rang. The Filipino boy glanced at Druse, Druse nodded, said: "Ask the gentleman to come in here." The Filipino boy went out and there were voices in the entrance-hall, and then Hanan came into the doorway.

Druse stood up. He said: "You must forgive us for beginning—you are a little late." He raised one hand and gestured towards the empty chair.

Hanan was standing in the doorway with his feet wide apart, his arms stiff at his sides, as if he had been suddenly frozen in that position. He stared at Mrs Hanan and his eyes were wide, blank—his thin mouth was compressed to a hard, straight line. Very suddenly his right hand went towards his left armpit.

Druse said sharply: "Please sit down." Though he seemed scarcely to have moved, the blunt derringer glittered in his hand.

Mrs Hanan half rose. She was very pale; her hands were clenched convulsively on the white tablecloth.

Hanan dropped his hand very slowly. He stared at the derringer and twisted his mouth into a terribly forced smile, came slowly forward to the empty chair and sat down.

Druse raised his eyes to the Filipino boy who had followed Hanan into the doorway, said: "Take the gentleman's gun, Tony—and serve his cocktail." He sat down, held the derringer rigidly on the table in front of him.

The Filipino boy went to Hanan, felt gingerly under his coat, drew out a small black automatic and took it to Druse. Then he went out through the swinging-door to the kitchen. Druse put the automatic in his pocket. He turned his eyes to Mrs Hanan, said: "I'm going to tell you a story. After I've finished, you can both talk all you like—but please don't interrupt."

He smiled with his mouth—the rest of his face remained stonily impassive. His eyes were fixed and expressionless, on Hanan. He said: "Your husband has wanted a divorce for some time. His principal reason is a lady—her name doesn't matter—who wants to marry him—and whom he wants to marry. He hasn't told you about her because he has felt, perhaps justifiably, that your knowing about her would retard, rather than hasten, an agreement. . . ."

The Filipino boy came in from the kitchen with a cocktail, set it before Hanan. Hanan did not move, or look up. He stared intently at the flowers in the center of the table. The Filipino boy smiled self-consciously at Druse and Mrs Hanan, disappeared into the kitchen.

Druse relaxed a little, leaned back; the derringer was still focused unwaveringly on Hanan.

"In the hope of uncovering some adequate grounds for bringing suit," Druse went on, "he has had you followed for a month or more—unsuccessfully, need I add? After you threatened Crandall, you discovered suddenly that you were being followed and, of course, ascribed it to Crandall."

He paused. It was entirely silent for a moment, except for the faint, faraway buzz of the city and the sharp, measured sound of Hanan's breathing.

Druse turned his head towards Mrs Hanan. "After you left Mister Hanan at Roslyn, last night, it suddenly occurred to him that this was his golden opportunity to dispose of you, without any danger to himself. You wouldn't give him a divorce—and it didn't look as if he'd be able to force it by discovering some dereliction on your part. And now, you had threatened Crandall—Crandall would be logically suspected if anything happened to you. Mister Hanan sent his men—the men who had been following you—after you when you left the place at Roslyn. They weren't very lucky."

Druse was smiling slightly. Mrs Hanan had put her elbows on the table, her chin in her hands; she regarded Hanan steadily.

"He couldn't go to the police," Druse went on—"they

116

would arrest Crandall, or watch him, and that would ruin the whole plan. And the business about the rubies would come out. That was the last thing he wanted"—Druse widened his smile—"because he switched the rubies himself—some time ago."

Mrs Hanan turned to look at Druse; very slowly she matched his smile.

"You never discovered that your rubies were fake," he said, "because that possibility didn't occur to you. It was only after they'd been given back by Crandall that you became suspicious and found out they weren't genuine." He glanced at Hanan and the smile went from his face, leaving it hard and expressionless again. "Mister Hanan is *indeed* 'crazy about stones.' "

Hanan's thin mouth twitched slightly; he stared steadily at the flowers.

Druse sighed. "And so—we find Mister Hanan, last night, with several reasons for wishing your—shall we say, disappearance? We find him with the circumstance of being able to direct suspicion at Crandall, ready to his hand. His only serious problem lay in finding a third, responsible, party before whom to lay the whole thing—or enough of it to serve his purpose."

Mrs Hanan had turned to face Hanan. Her eyes were half closed and her smile was very hard, very strange.

Druse stood up slowly, went on: "He had the happy thought of calling me—or perhaps the suggestion. I was an ideal instrument, functioning as I do, midway between the law and the underworld. He made an appointment, and arranged for one of his men to call on you by way of the fire-escape, while we were discussing the matter. The logical implication was that I would come to you when I left him, find you murdered, and act immediately on the information he had given me about Crandall. My influence and testimony would have speedily convicted Crandall. Mister Hanan would have better than a divorce. He'd have the rubies, without any danger of his having switched them ever being discovered—and he'd have"—Druse grinned sourly—"the check he had given me as an advance. Failing in the two things I had contracted to do, I would of course return it to him."

117

Hanan laughed suddenly; a terribly forced, high-pitched laugh.

"It is very funny," Druse said. "It would all have worked very beautifully if you"—he moved his eyes to Mrs Hanan—"hadn't happened to see the man who came up the fire-escape to call on you, before he saw you. The man whose return Mister Hanan has been impatiently waiting. The man"—he dropped one eyelid in a swift wink—"who confessed to the whole thing a little less than an hour ago."

Druse put his hand into his inside pocket and took out the black velvet jewel-case, snapped it open and put it on the table. "I found them in the safe at your place at Roslyn," he said. "Your servants there objected very strenuously—so strenuously that I was forced to tie them up and lock them in the wine cellar. They must be awfully uncomfortable by now—I shall have to attend to that."

He lowered his voice to a discreet drone. "And your lady was there, too. She, too, objected very strenuously, until I had had a long talk with her and convinced her of the error of her—shall we say, affection, for a gentleman of your instincts. She seemed very frightened at the idea of becoming involved in this case—I'm afraid she will be rather hard to find."

Druse sighed, lowered his eyes slowly to the rubies, touched the largest of them delicately with one finger. "And so," he said, "to end this vicious and regrettable business—I give you your rubies"—he lifted his hand and made a sweeping gesture towards Mrs Hanan—"and your wife—and now I would like your check for twenty-five thousand dollars."

Hanan moved very swiftly. He tipped the edge of the table upward, lunged up and forward in the same movement; there was a sharp, shattering crash of chinaware and silver. The derringer roared, but the bullet thudded into the table. Hanan bent over suddenly—his eyes were dull, and his upper lip was drawn back over his teeth—then he straightened and whirled and ran out through the door to the living room.

Mrs Hanan was standing against the big buffet; her hands were at her mouth, and her eyes were very wide. She made no sound.

Druse went after Hanan, stopped suddenly at the door. Hanan was crouched in the middle of the living room. The Filipino boy stood beyond him, framed against the darkness of the entrance-hall; a curved knife glittered in his hand and his thin yellow face was hard, menacing. Hanan ran out on the terrace and Druse went swiftly after him. By the dim light from the living room he saw Hanan dart to the left, encounter the wall there, zigzag crazily towards the darkness of the outer terrace, the edge.

Druse yelled: "Look out!" ran forward, Hanan was silhouetted a moment against the mauve glow of the sky; then with a hoarse, cracked scream he fell outward, down.

Druse stood a moment, staring blindly down. He took out a handkerchief and mopped his forehead, then turned and went into the living room and tossed the derringer down on the big center table. The Filipino boy was still standing in the doorway. Druse nodded at him and he turned and went through the dark entrance-hall into the kitchen. Druse went to the door to the dining room; Mrs Hanan was still standing with her back to the buffet, her hands still at her mouth, her eyes wide, unseeing. He turned and went swiftly up the broad steps to the office, took up the telephone and dialed a number. When the connection had been made, he asked for MacCrae.

In a minute or so MacCrae answered; Druse said: "You'll find a stiff in Mrs Dale Hanan's apartment on the corner of Sixty-third and Park, Mac. She killed him—self-defense. You might find his partner downstairs at my place—waiting for his boss to come out. . . . Yeah, his boss was Hanan—he just went down—the other way. . . . I'll file charges of attempted murder against Hanan, and straighten it all out when you get over here. . . . Yeah—hurry."

He hung up and went down to the dining room. He tipped the table back on its legs and picked up the rubies, put them back into the case. He said: "I called up a friend of mine who works for Mahlon and Stiles. As you probably know, Mister Hanan has never made a will." He smiled. "He so hated the thought of death that the idea of a will was extremely repugnant to him."

He picked up her chair and she came slowly across and sank into it.

119

"As soon as the estate is settled," he went on. "I shall expect your check for a hundred and thirty-five thousand dollars, made out to the insurance company."

She nodded abstractedly.

"I think these"—he indicated the jewel-case—"will be safer with me, until then."

She nodded again.

He smiled. "I shall also look forward with a great deal of pleasure to receiving your check for twenty-five thousand— the balance on the figure I quoted for my services."

She turned her head slowly, looked up at him. "A moralist," she said—"morbid—and mercenary."

"Mercenary as hell!" He bobbed his big head up and down violently.

She looked at the tiny watch at her wrist, said: "It isn't morning yet, strictly speaking—but I'd rather have a drink than anything I can think of."

Druse laughed. He went to the buffet and took out a squat bottle, glasses, poured two big drinks. He took one to her, raised the other and squinted through it at the light. "Here's to crime."

They drank.

The man in the dark-brown camel's-hair coat turned east against the icy wind. Near First Avenue he cut diagonally across the deserted street towards an electric sign: Tony Maschio's Day and Night Tonsorial Parlor.

A step or so beyond the sign, just outside the circle of warm yellow light from the shop, he stopped and put down the suitcase he was carrying, produced a cigarette and a lighter. He stood close to the building with his back to the wind, flicked the lighter several times without producing a flame, then turned back into the wind and went on towards First Avenue.

He forgot his suitcase. It sat in the darkness just under the corner of Tony's plate-glass window and if anyone had been close enough to it they might have heard it ticking between screaming gusts of wind—merrily, or ominously, depending upon whether one took it for the ticking of a cheap alarm clock or the vastly more intricate and alarming tick of a time-bomb.

The man walked up First Avenue to Thirteenth. He got into a cab on the northwest corner, said, "Grand Central," and leaned back and looked at his watch.

It was nine minutes after one.

At sixteen minutes after one Tony Maschio came out of the backroom, washed his hands, whistling a curiously individual version of "O Sole Mio," and turned to grin cheerily at the big bald man who sat reading a paper with his feet propped up on the fender of the stove.

"You are next, Mister Maccunn," he chirped brightly.

Tony Maschio looked like a bird, a white-faced bird with a bushy halo of black feathers on his head; he spoke with an odd twittering lilt, like a bird.

Maccunn folded his paper carefully and unfolded his big body as careful from the chair, stood up. He was about fifty-five, a very heavily built, heavily jowled Scot with glistening shoe-button eyes, a snow-white walrus mustache.

He lumbered over and sat down in Number One Chair, observed in a squeaky voice that contrasted strangely with his bulk:

"It's a cold, cold night."

For eight years Maccunn had come to Tony's every Friday night at around this time; for eight years his greeting, upon being invited into Tony's chair, had been: "It's a cold night," or "It's a hot night," or "It's a wet night," or whatever the night might be. When it was any of these things to an extreme degree he would repeat the adjectives in honor of the occasion. Tony agreed that it was a "cold, cold night" and asked his traditional question in turn, with a glittering smile:

"Haircut?"

Maccunn did not have so much as a pin-feather hair on his broad and shining head. He shook it soberly, as was his eight-year habit, closed his eyes, and Tony took up his shears and began trimming the enormous mustache with deft and graceful gusto.

Angelo, who presided over Number Two Chair, was industriously shaving the slack chin of a slight gray-faced youth in overalls. Giuseppe, Number Three, had gone out for something to eat. Giorgio, Number Four, was sitting in his chair, nodding over an ancient number of "The New Art Models Weekly." There were no other customers in the shop.

At nineteen minutes after one the telephone rang.

Maschio put down his shears and comb and started to answer it.

Angelo said: "If that's for me, boss—tell her to wait a minute."

Maschio nodded and put his hand out towards the receiver, and the telephone and wall came out to meet him, the whole side of the shop twisted and curled and was a smothering sheet of white flame, and pain. He felt his body torn apart as if it were being torn slowly and he thought "God!—please stop it!"—and then he didn't feel any more, or think any more.

Maccunn raised his head once and looked down at the

122

right side of his chest and it seemed curiously flat, curiously distant; he lowered his head and was still. Angelo moaned.

The wind was like an icy wall.

In the reporters' room of the Ninth Precinct Police Station, Nick Green was playing cooncan with Blondie Kessler, when the Desk Sergeant yelled from the next room:

"Blondie! Pineapple at Tony Maschio's Barber Shop on Seventh—nothin' left but a grease-spot!"

Kessler put his cards face down on the table and stood up slowly.

He said very simply: "Dear, sweet Jesus!"

Green looked up at him with elaborately skeptical disdain. "Every time I get a swell hand," he muttered plaintively, "something happens so you have an excuse to run out on me."

Kessler, moving towards the door, yipped: "Come on."

Nicholas, sometimes "St. Nick," Green was thirty-six—with the smooth tanned skin, bright China-blue eyes of twenty, the snowy white hair of sixty. He was tall and slim and angular, and his more or less severe taste in clothes was violently relieved by a predilection for flaming-red neckties.

His nickname derived from his rather odd ideas about philanthropy. He had been at one time or another a tent-show actor, a newspaperman, gambler, gun-runner, private detective and a few more ill-assorted what-nots, and that wide experience had given him decidedly revolutionary convictions as to who was deserving and who was not.

A stroke of luck combined with one of his occasional flashes of precise intuition had enabled him to snatch a fortune from a falling stock-market and for three years he had used his money and the power it carried to do most of the things young millionaires don't do. He numbered legmen, Park Avenue debutantes, pickpockets, touts, bank robbers and bank presidents, wardheelers and international confidence-men among his wide and varied circle of friends, and he had played Santa Claus to more than a few of them at one time or another. He found the devious twistings and turnings of politics, the complicated intrigues of the New York underworld exciting, spent more of his time in night courts than in night-clubs and was a great deal prouder of his accuracy with a Colt .45 than he was of his polo.

He got up and followed Blondie Kessler out of the Reporters' Room and down the corridor. In his car—a black and shiny and powerful coupé—they careened around the corner and roared north. Green swerved to miss a sleepily meandering cab by inches, asked:

"Now, about this Maschio?"

Blondie was a police-reporter on the Star-Telegram. His hair was as black as St. Nick's was white. He was a squat stocky Dutchman almost as broad as he was long and he had a habit of staccato, almost breathless expression, particularly when he was a little excited.

"Tony Maschio is—or was—Gino's brother. He's run a barber shop where a lot of the town's big shots go to have their fringes trimmed for eleven or twelve years, an' he's been partners with Gino an' Lew Costain in a high-powered gambling syndicate on the side. His shop was a little bit of a two-by-four joint, but Tony an' his hand-picked barbers were artists and it was usually full of names from Wall Street or Park Row."

Kessler was silent a moment; and Green invited: "And . . ."

"And—Bruce Maccunn, my Managing Editor, has been dropping in at Tony's for a mustache trim an' a mudpack every Friday night for as long as I can remember. I've located him there a half-dozen times in the last two or three years—late Friday nights."

Green whistled softly. "And . . ."

Kessler had no time to answer; the car slid to the curb across the street from the pile of smoking ruins that had been Maschio's Barber Shop. In spite of the hour, the glacial wind, the usual gallery of morbidly curious had gathered. Several firemen, policemen, and an ambulance squad from the Emergency Hospital were industriously combing the debris of bricks and steel and charred wood.

Kessler was the first reporter on the scene; he scurried about from one to another after information. Green strolled over to join two men who were standing a little way down the street in earnest conversation. One of them was Doyle, a plainclothesman whom he knew slightly, and the other was a wild-eyed Italian who was explaining with extravagant gestures that if he hadn't lingered in the corner lunch-room for a second cup of coffee he, too, would have been blown to bits. He, it appeared, was Giuseppe Picelli, Tony's Number Three Barber, and he'd been on his way back to the shop when the explosion occurred.

Green jerked his head towards the heap of wreckage. "How many have they found?"

"Don't know." Doyle chewed his unlighted cigar noisily. "Most of 'em are in pieces—little pieces. We've identified Tony an' one of his barbers, but there's a lot of pieces left over. This guy"—he nodded at Picelli—"says Bruce Maccunn was there—came in jus' before he left."

Picelli bobbed his head up and down, jabbered excitedly: "Sure, Mister Maccunn came in as I went out—an' there was another fellow—I don't know him. . . . An' Tony an' Angelo an' Giorgio . . ."

"That all?" Green was blowing hard in his bare hands to warm them.

"That's all were there when I left—but Gino an' Mister Costain were coming over. Tony was expecting them. . . ."

Green and Doyle looked at each other.

Doyle grunted: "If Lew Costain got there for the blow-off it makes my job about eight hundred percent harder. I don't guess there are more than eight hundred people in New York that'd like to see him in little pieces."

Kessler galloped over. He was a little green around the mouth and eyes.

"Mac g-got it!" he stuttered. "They just dug him out—or wh-what's left of him. . . ."

Doyle tried to light his cigar in the screaming wind. "Why did Gino Maschio an' Costain get it," he growled. "Maybe there's not enough left of them to find out, but if Picelli here knows his potatoes they were in the shop or on their way to the shop—an' if they were on their way they would've showed up by now."

Kessler gurgled: "Where's a telephone?"

"There's one in the lunchroom around the corner on Second Avenue." Picelli waved his arm dramatically.

A police car, its siren moaning shrilly, pulled up and a half dozen assorted detectives piled out.

Kessler grabbed Green's arm, shouted, "Come on, Nick—I gotta telephone an' I wanna talk to you." They hurried towards Second Avenue.

Green grinned down at the tugging, puffing reporter.

"You look like a crazed bloodhound," he said. "Don't tell me you've got another one of those red-hot Kessler theories."

"Theory my eye! I've got the whole business—the whole bloody shebang!"

"Uh-huh." Green's grunt was elaborately incredulous.

Kessler snorted. "Listen, John Sallust was released from Atlanta three days ago!"

"So what?"

Kessler's mouth made an amazed O. "So what! So Bruce Maccunn was the man who rode Sallust—in the paper—an' finally stuck him for the Arbor Day Parade bombing nearly five years ago. So Sallust swore by the beards of Marx and Lenin he'd get Maccunn. So, after a half-dozen appeals and new trials and whatnot he finally got a commutation and what does he do but make good and plant a pineapple under the man who put him behind the bars!"

They turned the corner.

Green murmured softly: "Blondie, my child—you're just as dippy as a bedbug—an especially dippy bedbug."

Kessler stopped suddenly, stood with his arms expressively outstretched and said:

"For the love of God—do you mean to tell me you don't get it? Maccunn, more than anyone else, or all the rest of 'em put together, hung that rap on Sallust. The Government wanted to drop the case on insufficient evidence, but Maccunn hated radicals like poison an' wouldn't let 'em. His editorials yelled about corruption and anarchy and it finally worked. What's more natural than Sallust wanting to wipe Maccunn as soon as he got out?"

Green shook his head slowly. "Nothing's more natural," he admitted. "Only I happen to know Sallust a little and he's much too bright a guy to do anything like this three days after he's sprung—or any other time."

Kessler's mouth flattened to a thin, sarcastic line.

"I followed his case very closely," Green went on, "and he was railroaded if anybody ever was. He's really a swell

126

guy who has his own ideas about the way the country should be run. I'll bet he never saw a bomb in his life."

"Nuts." Kessler half turned. "It all fits like a glove. He's an anarchist an' those boys say it with dynamite. He couldn't blow up the whole paper—that was too big an order—and Maccunn never lit long enough at his home for that to be practical, but he went to Tony Maschio's every Friday night between twelve-thirty and one-thirty. It's open and shut."

Green smiled sadly, shook his head, murmured: "Mostly shut."

"That's my story an' I'll stick to it." Kessler turned and went into the lunchroom.

Green walked slowly back towards his car, whispered into the wind:

"An especially dippy bedbug."

The hands of the big clock over the information desk pointed to one forty-one. The great concourse of Grand Central Station was speckled with the usual scattered crowd.

On the wide balcony above the west side of the concourse, the man in the dark-brown camel's-hair coat who had forgotten his suitcase in front of Tony Maschio's walked slowly back and forth. The collar of his coat was turned up and his hands were thrust deep in his pockets; his large dark eyes were fixed on Gate Twenty-seven, which led to the one-forty-five Boston train, and his head turned slowly as he walked back and forth.

He was a powerfully built man of uncertain age and as much of his face as could be seen above the heavy coat collar was unnaturally flushed.

Suddenly he stopped pacing and leaned forward against the marble balustrade. He had caught sight of a man of about his own build and coloring—moving swiftly across the concourse. The man's most striking features were the grace with which he moved and his bright yellowish-green velour hat. He flashed a ticket in front of the conductor and disappeared through Gate Twenty-seven.

The man in the dark-brown coat hurried down the great stairway, across to one of the ticket windows. When he

127

turned away he held a little piece of pasteboard and he strode with it through Gate Twenty-seven. He walked the length of the train to the first coach back of the baggage car and swung aboard.

He found the man he was looking for in the smoking car of the third Pullman back. There was no one else in the smoking room; the porter was making up a berth at the other end of the car.

The man in the dark-brown coat held the curtain aside with one arm and leaned against the side of the narrow doorway.

He said: "Hello."

The other swarthy man was sitting next to the window, reading a paper. He put the paper down and looked up and his color changed slowly, curiously, until his face was almost as yellow and as green as his jauntily cocked hat. He did not speak.

From outside, the conductor's voice came in to them: "All aboard. . . ."

The man in the dark-brown coat smiled a little; he whispered:

"Let's walk back and look at the lights."

The train began to move, slowly.

The other man's empty eyes were on one of the big pockets of the brown coat where something besides the big man's hand bulged the material. He did not move, seemed incapable of moving.

The man in the brown coat repeated: "Let's walk back. . . ." Then he crossed swiftly and grabbed the other's coat-collar with his free hand and jerked him to his feet, shoved him to the door and out into the narrow corridor; they went towards the rear of the train.

They went through four cars, most of them with the berths made up and curtains drawn, encountered only a heavily breathing drunk in pajamas who had mislaid something, and two sleepy porters. The last car was partly compartments, partly observation car. As they entered it, a red-haired brakeman passed them without looking at them and went forward. They went to the observation rear end and the man in the green hat said: "This is far enough, Lew, if you want to talk."

The man in the brown coat smiled. His right hand moved the coat pocket suggestively. He nodded his head sidewise, grunted, "Out on the platform, Gino. Then no one will hear us."

Gino took one glance at the bulged coat pocket, and opened the door to the observation platform.

The train was just coming out of the tunnel to the elevated tracks and the rosy glow of midtown Manhattan was reflected by the gray wind-driven clouds. The wind slashed like an icy knife and green-hat mechanically turned up his collar, shivered violently.

Following him, the man in the brown coat pulled the door shade down—both window shades were drawn—and closed the door tightly. He jerked his hand from his pocket. There was a momentary flash of something bright and glittering as he swung his hand up and down in a short arch against the other's skull. The hat went whirling away into the wind and darkness and the man sank to his knees, toppled forward to crush his face against the floor.

The man in the brown coat knelt beside him and went through his pockets swiftly, carefully. In the inside pocket of his suitcoat he found a thick packet of currency, slipped it into his own inside pocket.

A new sound, the faint stutter of an incoming train on the adjoining track, grew above the roar of the wind. The man glanced ahead, around the corner of the car, seemed for a moment to be calculating the distance away of the approaching headlight, then stooped again, swiftly.

Hurriedly he stripped off the man's overcoat, then his own. He struggled into the former—a rather tight-fitting tweed Chesterfield—and somehow forced the other man's arms and shoulders into his own big dark-brown camel's hair; then he finished transferring the contents of his own inside pockets—several letters, a monogrammed cigarette case and other odds and ends—to the inside pockets of the unconscious man.

The stutter of the approaching train grew to a hoarse scream. He boosted the limp body onto his shoulder, stood up, and when the blinding headlight of the train on the adjoining track was about twenty-five or thirty feet away, he dumped his burden over the side-rail of the observation platform down onto the track in front of the onrushing locomotive.

Then he turned swiftly and went back through the observation car. As he reached the third car forward the train slowed and he heard a far-off voice shout:

"Hundred an' Twenty-fifth Street."

When the train stopped and a porter opened the doors of the vestibule between the third and fourth car, the man, now in a tight-fitting tweed Chesterfield, swung off and sauntered down the stairs that led from the station to the street.

As he crossed the street towards a cab he heard the conductor's thin far off wail above the wind: "All aboard. . . ."

He climbed into the cab, snapped: "Three thirty-two West Ninetieth—and make it fast."

Green lit a match and examined the mailboxes carefully. The second one on the left rewarded him with a dingy label upon which:

JOHN DARRELL SALLUST
PAULA SALLUST

had been typewritten in bright-blue ink.

He rang the bell under the label and after a minute the lock of the outside door buzzed; he went in and climbed two flights of narrow stairs to Apartment B5. The door was ajar; he knocked and a man's high-pitched voice called:

"Come in."

Green went into a very large and bare studio, dimly lighted by two floor-lamps in opposite corners and a small but very bright desk lamp on a wide central table.

The high-pitched voice: "Well, Mister Green—this is an unexpected pleasure."

Green took off his hat and went to the wide table. He bowed slightly.

"Might you, by any chance," he inquired blandly, "have been out this evening—since, say eleven o'clock?"

John Sallust was a thin, consumptive-looking Englishman with a high bulging forehead, stringy mouse-colored hair, and cold gray eyes, so light in color that they appeared almost white. He sat straddling a chair, his chin resting on his clasped hands on the back of the chair.

"I not only might have," he said evenly—"I was. I only got home about a quarter of an hour ago."

Green glanced at the square heavy watch on the inside of his left wrist; it was fifty-two minutes after one.

Sallust turned his head. "This is Paula, my sister. This is Nick Green. You've probably heard me speak of him."

She was half sitting, half lying on a low couch against one of the long walls of the room, a very dark, very diminutive girl with porcelain-white skin, a deep-red mouth and large oddly opaque eyes.

She nodded and Green bowed again slightly.

"We went to a theater." She sat up slowly. "We went to a theater and John brought me home afterwards—it must have been about ten-thirty—and then he went for a walk."

Green smiled. "That's simply dandy. Now, if you two can jump into your hats and coats and the three of us can get out of here in about one minute flat"—he raised one snowy eyebrow and grinned at Sallust—"you won't have to take another of those very unpleasant trips to jail."

Paula leapt to her feet, almost screamed: "Jail!"

Sallust's thin face twisted to a wry smile. "You choose a rather bizarre time to joke, Mister Green," he said softly.

Green was looking at his watch. "Maybe in two minutes," he whispered as if to himself.

Paula crossed to him swiftly.

"What are you talking about?" she gulped. "What is it?"

"I haven't time to tell you about it, now. Take my word for it that the Law will be here in a split-jiffy to arrest your brother for the murder of Bruce Maccunn and a half-dozen or so innocent bystanders. Let's go first and talk about it afterwards. . . ."

Sallust did not move. His eyes moved swiftly to his sister once, then back to Green.

He muttered: "No."

Green stared at him blankly. "No? No what?"

Sallust shook his head a little. "I returned three days ago," he said gently, "from the better part of five years in prison. I was as I believe you call it, framed. I was accused by lies, tried by lies, convicted by lies. . . ."

131

He cleared his throat and straightened in the chair, gazed very intently at Green.

"I know you very slightly, Mister Green. I have been led to believe at one time or another that you are in some way sympathetic to our cause, but I have just returned from a painful five-year lesson in misplaced trust. I do not know what you are talking about, now, but I know that I have done no wrong and I shall stay exactly where I am."

It was entirely silent for a moment and then Paula's voice rang softly, tremulously: "Perhaps you're making a mistake, John. Mister Green is—" She stopped.

Green put his hand up and rubbed the heel of it slowly down the left side of his face. His eyes were fixed more or less vacantly on a small turkey-red cigarette box on the table. Very suddenly he went forward and as Sallust sprang to his feet, Green's arm moved in a long looping arc, his knuckles smacked sharply against Sallust's chin; Sallust crumpled and fell to his knees, clutched blindly at the chair, went limp.

Paula was too surprised to scream, or move; she stood with her hands to her mouth, her great eyes fixed on Green in startled amazement.

Green mumbled, "Sorry," shortly, stooped and swept Sallust's slight figure up into his arms and moved towards the door. "Come on," he grunted over his shoulder, "and make it snappy."

She followed in stunned silence; at the door he turned and jerked his head at her coat and she took it up from a chair and put it on like a somnambulist motivated and moved by something unknown, something irresistible.

The bleak Greenwich Village street was deserted; Green carried Sallust across the glistening sidewalk and put him in the car, hurried around to climb in behind the wheel. Paula stood hesitantly on the sidewalk; the cold air had brought back her momentarily dimmed senses and she reflected that it was not too late to scream, reflected further, after glancing up and down the street, that it was more or less useless. She got into the car and closed the door, put her arm around Sallust and waited.

Just east of Eighth Avenue, Green slowed and pulled

over to the curb to allow two speeding police-cars to pass, then turned and watched them skid to the curb outside the building where the Sallusts lived.

He grinned at Paula. "My timing wasn't so hot," he observed. "The Law was about three minutes less efficient than I figured."

She turned from watching the men swarm out of the cars and run into the house. Her inclination to scream was definitely gone; she tried to return his smile.

"What is it all about?" she whispered. "I don't understand . . ."

"Neither do I yet." He let the clutch in and the car rounded the corner, whirred north on Eighth Avenue. "I'm sorry I had to resort to that to get your brother out, but I thought he got a raw deal before and I want to do what I can to prevent his getting another one. After five years on the inside he shouldn't mind a sock on the jaw if it saves him even one night in the cooler."

Green's apartment was on East Sixty-first; the elevator boy helped him with Sallust, who was beginning to stir and moan feebly; Green explained that he was very drunk and when they reached his apartment on the top floor they put Sallust on one of the divans in the huge living room. The elevator boy went away.

Green turned to Paula. "He'll be all right in a little while," he said. "The main thing is that he's not to show up outside of this place until certain matters—I'm not quite sure what, yet, so I can't tell you about them—are straightened out. Do you trust me enough to help, and to see to it that he stays here?"

She nodded.

Green smiled slightly. "Your word?"

She nodded again, returned the faint shadow of a smile.

He went towards the door. "I'll be back or give you a ring as soon as I can. Make yourself at home. If you get hungry or thirsty try the icebox."

He went out and closed the door.

Downstairs, he admonished the night clerk. "There're a man and woman in my apartment and I want them to stay there. I think they will, but if they get tough call Mike and let him handle them."

The clerk nodded; he was accustomed to more or less curious orders from Mister Green. Mike was the janitor, a husky Norwegian who had performed odd jobs of a strong-arm nature for Green upon more than one occasion.

Green turned in the doorway. "And if they make any telephone calls, keep a record of who they call and what they have to say."

The clerk nodded again. Green went out into Sixty-first Street and walked to a drugstore.

At eighteen minutes after two the phone on Blondie Kessler's desk jingled cheerily for the tenth time in twenty-five minutes.

He whirled from his typewriter, picked up the receiver and yelped: "Hello."

Green's voice hummed silkily over the wire:

"How many more identifiable pieces have they dug out of Tony's? And how's that red-hot Kessler theory coming along?"

Kessler scowled sourly into the transmitter.

"That Kessler theory is holding its head up and taking nourishment very nicely, thank you!" he barked with elaborate irony. "We found a chunk of the fuse with a foundry label on it, a place in Jersey—"

Green interrupted: "Don't tell me. Let me guess. . . . Sallust used to work there, or anyway, he used to live in Jersey, or maybe he went to Jersey once to visit his aunt."

Kessler snorted: "All right, all right. I say Sallust is a cinch for this job, you say not. I'll bet—I'll bet you fifty dollars."

Green snapped: "Bet."

Kessler cackled shrilly. "The clincher is that Sallust and his sister took a powder about a minute and a half before the boys in blue swept in. Their next-door neighbors heard them go out and from the timing it looks like it was a tip."

Green sighed. "Maybe I'm the bedbug, after all," he murmured. "And how about my first and most important question—what else have they dug up?"

"Nothing more that they could make sense of. They've got a lot of arms and legs that might have been Gino or Costain or who-have-you."

Green's voice droned on: "I'm still curious about

134

whether Gino and Costain got to Tony's before the fireworks. Has anybody tried to locate them?"

"Uh-huh. Gino was supposed to leave for Boston on a late train, after he went to Tony's. A business trip according to his wife. She don't know whether he reached Tony's or whether he made the train or not. She's going nuts. Then I reached Costain's girl and she said Lew started for Tony's about midnight, said he was going to stop by a couple places first. She hasn't heard from him since. She's jumping up and down and yelling and screaming, too, and calling me back every two minutes."

There was silence for several seconds, then Green's voice concluded dreamily:

"Don't forget, Blondie, that Lew Costain has, or had, more enemies than any other picked dozen highbinders in this town. Maccunn had one, or at least you're trying to hang his chill on one. Whether Costain reached Tony's or not, he was headed there, and in some strange way that seems more important to me than the fact that Sallust wanted Maccunn's blood. With all due respect to the Kessler theory, of course. . . . And don't forget the fifty. . . ."

The phone clicked, an electric period.

Kessler looked like he was going to take a large bite out of the transmitter for a minute, then he hung up slowly and turned back to his typewriter with enormous disgust.

Haley, the City Editor, was working feverishly, trying very hard not to whistle. He, for one, had hated Maccunn as a slave driver, and now it looked like he'd be moving into the big oak-paneled office on the seventh floor and be writing M.E. after his name.

He looked up as Kessler hung up the receiver, yelled: "Anything new?"

Kessler shook his head. "Nothing new, only that guy Green is losing his mind."

Solly Allenberg, short and fat, was sitting in his cab near the corner of Forty-ninth and Broadway, when Green crossed the street to him.

Allenberg stopped short in the middle of a yawn and his face lit up like a chubby Christmas tree.

"Hello, Mister Green," he croaked heartily. "Where you been keeping yourself?"

Green leaned on the door.

"I've been around," he said. "How've you been doing, Solly? How are the kids?"

"Swell, Mister Green, just swell. The wife was asking about you just the other night. I told her—"

Green interrupted quietly: "Lew Costain's been murdered."

Solly's thick mouth fell open slowly. "Murdered? What the hell you talking about?"

Green's head bobbed up and down.

"He was at Tony Maschio's tonight when the firecracker went off—he and Gino. . . ."

Solly said: "I was just reading about it in the paper, but it didn't say nothing about Mister Costain."

"They hadn't identified him when they snapped that Extra out."

Green reached past Solly and clicked down the taxi-meter flag. "Let's take a ride," he suggested—"only let's take it inside, where it's warm and where we can get a drink."

Solly tumbled out of the cab and they crossed the slippery sidewalk and went into the Rialto Bar. They both ordered rye. Green studied Solly's reflection in the big mirror behind the bar.

"How long have you been working for Lew?" he began. Solly hesitated and Green went on swiftly: "Listen. I knew him pretty well, liked him. I intend to find who rubbed him out and you can help me, if you will. . . ."

Solly gulped his drink. "Sure," he blurted—"I wanta help." He glanced at his empty glass and Green nodded to the bartender to fill it up.

"I never really worked for him," Solly went on. "He was scared of cars—scared to drive his own car in town. He got the batty idea two, three years ago I was a swell, careful driver, so he's been riding in my cab most of the time since. Whenever he'd light anywhere for awhile or go home an' go to bed or anything like that, he'd tell me an' I'd pick up what I could on the side. He paid me a flat rate of a sawbuck a day no matter what the meter read an' some days he wouldn't use me at all, so it worked out swell."

"Did you take him anywhere tonight?"

"Uh-huh." Solly drank, nodded. "I picked him up at his

apartment a little after midnight an' took him to the corner of Bleecker an' Thompson Street. He said he wouldn't need me any more tonight."

Green tasted his rye, made a face and put a twenty-dollar bill on the bar.

Solly said, "Don't you like it, Mister Green?"

Green shook his head and edged the glass along the bar with the side of his hand until it was in front of Solly.

Solly regarded it meditatively. "I'll be damned," he said, "a swell guy like Mister Costain getting the works like that. . . ." He picked up the glass.

Green was lighting a cigarette. "Who did it?"

Solly shrugged. "There is a lot of guys who never liked him, because they didn't understand him. He was—uh—ec—" Solly stopped, tasted his fresh drink and tried again: "He was ec—"

"Eccentric?"

Solly bobbed his head.

Green persisted: "But who hated him enough and had guts enough to tip him over?"

Solly drained his glass, then closed one eye and looked immeasurably wise. "Well, if you ask me," he said quickly, "the guy who had plenty of reason to, an' maybe enough guts to, was plenty close to home. . . . Did'ja ever meet a fella named Demetrios—something Demetrios? A Greek—tall shiny-haired sheik with a big smile?"

Green shook his head.

Solly leaned closer. "He worked as a kind of bodyguard an' all-around handy-man for Mister Costain. Mister Costain liked him. . . ." Solly's voice dissolved to a hoarse stage-whisper. "I happen to know that Demetrios an' June Neilan, Costain's girl, was like that"—he held up two grimy fingers pressed close together—"right under Costain's nose."

Green's brows ascended to twin inverted v's. "That's a good reason for Costain to hang it on the Greek," he objected, "but not the other way around."

"Wait a minute. You don't get it." Solly's face split to a wide grin. "I happen to know this Demetrios has tried to let Costain have it in the back a couple times, only it went wrong, an' Costain didn't even tumble to who it

137

was. I happened to be in the right place at the right time."

"Why didn't you tell Costain?"

Solly stared hard at his empty glass.

Green smiled faintly. "Did Demetrios pay off?"

Solly nodded sheepishly. Green rapped on the bar and the bartender filled both glasses.

"It's just like it always is," Solly croaked philosophically. "Costain was crazy jealous of everybody except the right guy, an' distrusted everybody except the guy who was holding the knife."

"Where did Costain live? Some place on West Ninetieth, wasn't it?"

"Uh-huh. Three thirty-one."

Green picked up his change and Solly gulped both drinks and they went out and started across the slippery sidewalk towards the cab.

A slight, white-faced man with his coat collar turned up and the brim of his soft black hat turned down as much as possible to cover his face came up to them and said, "Hello, Solly. Hello, Mister Green," in a soft muffled voice. He took a short snubnosed revolver out of his overcoat pocket and shot Solly in the stomach twice. Solly slipped and fell sidewise against Green and they both fell; Solly took two more slugs that were intended for Green. The cold magnified the roar of the gun to thunder. The wind whipped around the corner and the brim of the white-faced man's hat blew up and Green recognized Giuseppe Picelli, Number Three Barber.

Then Green and Solly were a tangled mass of threshing arms and legs on the icy sidewalk and Picelli turned and ran east on Forty-ninth Street.

On the third floor of the rooming house at Three Thirty-two West Ninetieth, directly across the street from Three Thirty-one, a man sat motionlessly at the window of the large dimly lighted front room. He had taken off the tweed Chesterfield he had worn when he left the Boston train at One Hundred and Twenty-fifth Street, and his suit coat; he sat in his deep-pink silk shirt-sleeves on the edge of a heavily upholstered chair, leaning forward to peer steadily through the slit under the drawn window shade.

From time to time he lighted a fresh cigarette from the butt of the last, glanced at his watch; these were the sole disturbances to his rigid immobility, his entirely silent vigil.

At two thirty-six the phone rang. He picked it up from the floor with his eyes on the slit, grunted: "Yeah."

He listened silently for perhaps a minute, then said: "What the hell difference does it make whether Green recognized you or not if he's dead? . . . Oh, you're not sure. They both fell, but you're not sure"—his tone dripped sarcasm—"Well, you'd better make sure. I don't care how you do it, you've had your orders. Check on it some way and then come on up here, and be careful when you come in."

He put the phone on the floor, lighted a fresh cigarette.

Demetrios said: "I don't know nothing about it."

Doyle glanced swiftly at the detective lieutenant who had accompanied him. "Well, we figured you'd want to know," he mumbled.

Demetrios pulled his bright yellow dressing-gown more closely around his shoulders, shivered slightly, nodded.

They were in Demetrios' small apartment on Seventy-sixth Street. He'd been in bed, asleep; Doyle and the lieutenant had pounded on the door for three or four minutes before they'd succeeded in waking him.

The detective lieutenant stood up, stretched, yawned extravagantly.

Someone knocked at the door.

Doyle opened it and Green came in. He nodded to Doyle and the lieutenant, jerked his head at Demetrios.

"I don't know this gent, but I want to have a little talk with him," he said. "Will somebody please introduce me?"

Demetrios stared at him unpleasantly. "Is this guy a dick?"

Doyle grinned, shook his head. "Huh-uh. This is St. Nick Green. He's a nice fella. You two ought to know each other."

Demetrios stood up angrily. "What the hell you mean coming into my house like this?" He whirled on Doyle and the lieutenant. "You, too. You got a warrant? I don't know nothing about Costain—"

Doyle clucked: "Tch, tch, such a temper!" He smiled

at Green. "Don't mind him. We woke him up an' he's pouting."

Green sat down on the arm of a chair.

"Speaking of Costain," he said softly, "has he turned up yet?" He turned to Doyle. "Something tells me he wasn't at Tony's and that he's still in one piece."

They were all looking at Green; Demetrios and the lieutenant with more or less puzzled expressions, Doyle with a broad grin.

Doyle laughed. "You're a little behind the times, Nicky," he boomed. "They found what was left of Costain on the New York Central tracks at a Hundred an' Twenty-first Street a little while ago. No mistake about it this time. He was identified by a lot of papers an' stuff in his pockets."

The lieutenant said: "That's why we woke up his nibs, here. We thought he might know something about it."

Demetrios turned and closed the window savagely. "I don't know nothing about it," he snarled. "I told Lew I didn't want no part of it. I been in bed since ten o'clock an' got a witness to prove it. There's been three phone calls through the switchboard, so the operator knows I was in."

Green asked gently: "Told Lew you didn't want any part of what?"

"Any part of nothing! Me an' him was washed up. He's been screwy for the last week. He thought everybody was trying to double-cross him."

Green purred: "Everybody probably was."

Doyle repeated: "Any part of what, Demetrios?"

Demetrios sat down. "He was tipped off yesterday that Gino an' Tony were juggling the books. One of Tony's barbers called him an' said instead of the syndicate going into the red like it's supposed to been going the last few weeks, it's been cleaning up important money. Costain never paid any attention to the business. He didn't have no head for figures. He furnished the original bankroll an' trusted Gino an' Tony to take care of the business."

The lieutenant muttered: "Christ, what a character shark! Trusting Gino and Tony!"

"They were going to take a powder, according to Lew's info," Demetrios went on. "Gino was going to shag a boat out of Boston for Havana an' Tony was going to Florida by rail an' meet him there. Between them they were supposed to have about four hundred grand. Lew told me about it an' said he'd made a date to meet both of them at Tony's at a quarter after one tonight. He wanted me to go along, but I couldn't see it. It looked like a dumb play. Anyway, me an' him was washed up and I been in bed since ten o'clock."

The lieutenant snapped: "You're good enough for us, Demetrios, as a material witness. Get on your clothes."

"That's what I get for trying to help you dumb bastards," Demetrios bleated. He got up and went into the bathroom.

Green stood up, crossed quietly to Doyle and the lieutenant, whispered: "Don't pick him up. Tell him to stand by for a call in the morning and let him go. I'll lay six, two, and even he doesn't go back to bed, but goes out. We can wait outside and if he doesn't lead us somewhere I'm a Tasmanian watchmaker."

Doyle looked doubtful, but the lieutenant seemed to like the idea.

He called: "Let it go, Demetrios. But stick around for a call in the morning."

Demetrios appeared in the bathroom doorway in his pajamas. He looked a little bewildered.

"Can I go back to bed?"

Doyle said: "Sure. Get some sleep. You'll probably need it. After all, we wouldn't be getting nowhere in figuring out what this's all about if it wasn't for you."

Demetrios nodded glumly, went over and sat down on the edge of the bed.

Doyle grunted, "G'night," and he and Green and the lieutenant filed out.

Demetrios sat silent for two or three minutes and then got up and went to the door, opened it and looked up and down the hall. Then he closed the door and crossed to the private telephone that stood on the stand beside the bed, beside the regular house phone. He sat down on the bed again and dialed a Schuyler number, said:

"Hello, honey. Listen. The big news just came through. They found 'im on the New York Central tracks, uptown. Uh-huh. I guess he left the pinwheel at Tony's an' picked up Gino on the Boston train. Only Gino saw him first. . . ."

A couple coppers just stopped by an' told me. They thought I might like to know."

He laughed quietly. "Sure, I gave 'em enough so they know he blasted Tony's. They can figure the rest of it out for themselves. Now, listen. They're probably waiting for me outside, but I'm going to duck out through the basement." He glanced at the alarm clock on the dresser. "It's a quarter of three. I'll be over there in half an hour at the outside unless they tail me an' then I'll have to lose 'em. You throw some things in a bag an' be ready to leave. We'll take a little trip. Some place where it's cool. . . . Okay, baby— 'Bye."

He hung up, dressed swiftly and took a traveling-bag out of a closet, began stuffing clothes into it.

Green's car was parked on the other side of Broadway, on Seventy-sixth. He went into an all-night drugstore on the corner and called the Star-Telegram, asked for Kessler.

Kessler grunted, "Hello," wearily, snapped out of it when he recognized Green's voice.

"Hey, Nick! I just heard somebody took a shot at you," he yelped. "You all right?"

"I'm okay. I'll tell you all about it when I see you."

"That's swell," Kessler whooped. "Everything's swell! I just put the Star-Telegram exclusive on Sallust to bed. What a story! It oughta be on the streets in an hour."

Green said softly: "Blondie, if you want to keep your job, and keep the Star out of an awful jam, kill it." Then, before Kessler could answer, he went on: "I just left Demetrios' apartment. He's the tall good-looking Greek that worked for Costain. Doyle and his partner are waiting for him to show, to tail him, but I'm afraid he'll get past them and I have a very merry hunch where he's going."

Kessler interrupted: "But listen, Nick—"

"You listen." Green's tone was ominous. "Hold that story for at least an hour, and leap up to Three Thirty-one West Ninetieth with some Law, fast. I'll be outside, or if I'm not, I'll be upstairs in Costain's apartment. Come up, and come quick. This is going to be the payoff on everything that's happened tonight and it'll make your Sallust story look like a want ad."

"But listen. . . ." Kessler sounded like he was about to cry.

Green snapped: "I'm depending on you. Make it fast and

142

make it quiet. And don't forget to bring along that fifty skins."

He hung up the receiver and went out and got into his car, drove to Amsterdam Avenue, up Amsterdam to Eighty-ninth, turned west. He parked just off Riverside Drive on Ninetieth, about a hundred and fifty feet west of the entrance to Three Thirty-one.

Then he lighted a cigarette and sat still and waited.

The man in the third-floor-front room at Three Thirty-two didn't smoke any more; he simply waited, his eyes at the slit under the window shade. Occasionally he leaned back in the big chair, but for only a few seconds at a time and only after ten minutes or so of rigid, wary immobility.

At four minutes after three someone knocked at the door. He got up and opened it swiftly. Giuseppe Picelli came in; the man went back to the window.

Picelli sat down, said dully: "Got Solly. Green got away. There was ice . . ."

"There was ice," the man at the window repeated slowly. "All right, there was ice. How long were they together?"

"Green came up to Solly—Solly was in his cab. They went into the bar and I called you. Two or three minutes after I came out of the booth, they came out. I went up to them on the sidewalk . . ."

"And there was ice."

The man at the window stiffened suddenly, shaded his eyes from the dim light in the room. He peered intently through the slit for perhaps ten or fifteen seconds, then stood up and picked up his suit-coat and put it on.

"Come on, Joe. We're going places," he said.

He took a big blue automatic out of the pocket of the tweed Chesterfield and stuck it against his stomach, under the belt, pulled the points of his vest down over it.

The two men went together out of the room and down two flights of stairs, out of the rooming house and across the street to Three Thirty-one.

The elevator boy stared wide-eyed at the man who had been sitting at the window.

"Jeeze, Mister Costain," he stuttered. "I thought—Miss Neilan has been going crazy—calling up the newspapers every few minutes . . ."

Costain did not answer.

They got off at the fourth floor, went to the door of the front apartment on the right. Costain took a bunch of keys out of his pocket and unlocked it, opened it. They went in and closed the door.

June Neilan was a very pretty platinum blonde with wide blue eyes, orange lips that looked as if they had been put on to stay. She turned and stared at Costain and her creamy skin went gray.

Demetrios' hand moved swiftly upward across his chest and then he looked at the snub-nosed revolver in Picelli's hand, changed his mind and dropped his hands to his side, slowly.

Costain said: "Sit down."

June Neilan walked unsteadily to the nearest chair, sat down. Demetrios stood still.

Costain went to Demetrios and reached inside his coat, jerked a .35 automatic out of a shoulder holster and handed it back to Picelli. Then he doubled up his right fist and swung hard at Demetrios' jaw. Demetrios moved backward a little and Costain's fist cut his cheek; two tiny drops of blood started out on the white skin just beneath the cheekbone.

Costain drew his fist back and swung again; this time his timing was better, there was a soft splat as his fist struck Demetrios' jaw, Demetrios reeled backward against the wall. Costain went after him, cocked his right again.

June Neilan said, "Please don't, Lew," dully.

Costain's right fist ripped into Demetrios' throat, his left smashed his nose. Demetrios made a curious strangling sound and slid sidewise down the wall to the floor.

Costain was panting, his heavy florid face was purple. He drew his foot back and kicked Demetrios' face, hard, again and again; it made a soft, smacking sound like someone snapping their fingers in water and Demetrios' face darkened with glistening deep-red blood.

Someone pounded on the door.

Costain did not seem to hear; he raised his foot and stamped on Demetrios' face so hard that the bones of the nose and cheek crunched like crumpled paper.

Picelli whimpered: "Boss—there's somebody outside. . . ."

Costain did not turn his head; he panted: "Okay—let 'em be outside. I'm busy. . . ."

The pounding came on the door again.

June Neilan was staring at Costain and Demetrios blindly; she jumped up suddenly and ran to the door. Picelli was a split-second too late. She turned the lock, the door swung open and Nick Green stood in the opening.

Costain turned from Demetrios and jerked the big automatic out of his belt, shot twice. June Neilan spun around as if a heavy unseen hand were on her shoulder, twisting her slight body.

Green felt the sleeve of his coat lift, tear, a hot stab of pain in the outer muscle of his left arm. He shot once from a little above the hip. Costain bent forward slowly as if in an extravagant bow; then he sank to one knee and raised his head, stared vacantly at June Neilan.

She was holding on to the edge of the door with her two hands. Her eyes went back in her head suddenly and her body folded; she fell.

Green came forward into the room.

Picelli was shivering violently and his face looked very pinched and small; his revolver fell to the floor and he raised his hands slowly.

Costain's mouth twisted upward a little to a kind of grin, he toppled sidewise and as he struck the floor he straightened his right arm until the muzzle of the big automatic was jammed into Demetrios' stomach.

The dark doorway was suddenly crowded with faces, men. Doyle and Kessler and two detectives from the Ninth Precinct Station came into the room. One of the detectives picked up Picelli's and Demetrios' guns, the other knelt beside June Neilan.

Doyle went past Green and stood looking down at Costain. Costain had emptied the big automatic into Demetrios' stomach; he rolled over and raised his head a little, grinned up at Doyle, then at Green.

"That was a good job," he whispered. "That was the best job I've ever done. . . ."

His head fell back. Doyle stooped over him.

"He'll be all right, I think," Green said slowly. "I tried to shoot him in the leg and in the shoulder. . . ." He turned to

Kessler with a very faraway expression on his face. "I wonder why."

The detective kneeling beside June Neilan looked up. "The gal hasn't got a scratch," he mumbled. "She bumped her head on the door when she fell but that's all."

Green said: "I guess she fainted. Costain's a lousy shot."

He peeled off his overcoat and his suit coat, sat down and rolled up his shirtsleeve. The wound on the arm was slight, a crease; one of the detectives wrapped a clean handkerchief around it and tied it.

Kessler was staring blankly at Costain. "I still don't get it," he stuttered. "How many times can you kill one guy? Who was the guy they—they found on the tracks?"

Doyle was at the phone.

Green smiled at Kessler. "That'd be Gino," he said. "Picelli tipped Costain that Gino and Tony were running out on him with all the syndicate's dough. Costain left the ticker at Tony's and then caught up with Gino on the late Boston train. He probably got the bright idea that if he made it look like he'd been killed he could sneak back to a spot where he could watch the apartment, he might catch Demetrios and his girl friend in the act."

Doyle hung up the receiver and turned to listen.

"He's probably been suspicious of them for a week or so," Green went on. "That was his reason for keeping away from her until Demetrios showed. He planted his things on Gino and tossed him under the train; he wasn't sure it'd work or how long it'd take for 'em to find what was left of Gino, so he called Picelli and told him to check on it. Picelli checked and sure enough, the report had gone out that Costain's body had been found. Then all Costain had to do was wait for Demetrios to turn up to break the big news to the girl."

Green rolled his shirtsleeve down and got up and put on his coat.

"Picelli shot Solly Allenberg tonight because Solly drove Costain to the corner of Bleecker and Thompson. That's about a half-block from where Maxie Sillmann lives and Maxie's the boy who specializes in plain and fancy pineapples. Costain wanted to be sure no one got to Solly because Solly knew a little bit too much about the whole business, and he probably had Picelli watching him. My guess is that Picelli called him back and told him Solly and I were in the bar and that I'd been at Tony's after the blast, so Costain told Picelli to let both of us have it."

Green was looking at Picelli. Picelli nodded slightly.

Kessler had perked up amazingly; he suddenly dashed for the telephone.

Green said: "Wait a minute, Blondie. I've get a couple of important calls to make."

He crossed to the telephone and sat down and called the Receiving Hospital, asked about Solly Allenberg. He waited a minute, then shook his head and whispered, "That's too bad," hung up the receiver and looked at Kessler.

"I'll take that fifty, now," he said softly.

VINTAGE CRIME / **BLACK LIZARD**

____ **Carny Kill** by Robert Edmond Alter $8.00   0-679-74443-6

____ **Swamp Sister** by Robert Edmond Alter $9.00   0-679-74442-8

____ **The Far Cry** by Fredric Brown $8.00   0-679-73469-4

____ **His Name Was Death** by Fredric Brown $8.00   0-679-73468-6

____ **No Beast So Fierce** by Edward Bunker $10.00   0-679-74155-0

____ **Double Indemnity** by James M. Cain $8.00   0-679-72322-6

____ **The Postman Always Rings Twice** $8.00   0-679-72325-0
  by James M. Cain

____ **The Big Sleep** by Raymond Chandler $9.00   0-394-75828-5

____ **Farewell, My Lovely** by Raymond Chandler $10.00   0-394-75827-7

____ **The High Window** $10.00   0-394-75826-9
  by Raymond Chandler

____ **The Lady in the Lake** by Raymond Chandler $10.00   0-394-75825-0

____ **The Long Goodbye** $10.00   0-394-75768-8
  by Raymond Chandler

____ **Trouble Is My Business** by Raymond Chandler $9.00   0-394-75764-5

____ **I Wake Up Screaming** by Steve Fisher $8.00   0-679-73677-8

____ **Black Friday** by David Goodis $7.95   0-679-73255-1

____ **The Burglar** by David Goodis $8.00   0-679-73472-4

____ **Cassidy's Girl** by David Goodis $8.00   0-679-73851-7

____ **Night Squad** by David Goodis $8.00   0-679-73698-0

____ **Nightfall** by David Goodis $8.00   0-679-73474-0

____ **Shoot the Piano Player** $7.95   0-679-73254-3
  by David Goodis

____ **Street of No Return** by David Goodis $8.00   0-679-73473-2

____ **The Continental OP** $10.00   0-679-72258-0
  by Dashiell Hammett

____ **The Maltese Falcon** $9.00   0-679-72264-5
  by Dashiell Hammett

____ **Red Harvest** by Dashiell Hammett $9.00   0-679-72261-0

____ **The Thin Man** by Dashiell Hammett $9.00   0-679-72263-7

____ **Ripley Under Ground** by Patricia Highsmith $10.00   0-679-74230-1

____ **The Talented Mr. Ripley** by Patricia Highsmith $10.00   0-679-74229-8

____ **A Rage in Harlem** by Chester Himes $8.00   0-679-72040-5

____ **The Name of the Game is Death** $9.00   0-679-73848-7
  by Dan Marlowe

____ **Shattered** by Richard Neely $9.00   0-679-73498-8

VINTAGE CRIME / **BLACK LIZARD**

____ **Kill the Boss Good-bye** by Peter Rabe	$9.00	0-679-74069-4
____ **The Laughing Policeman** by Maj Sjöwall and Per Wahlöö	$9.00	0-679-74223-9
____ **The Locked Room** by Maj Sjöwall and Per Wahlöö	$10.00	0-679-74222-0
____ **The Man on the Balcony** by Maj Sjöwall and Per Wahlöö	$9.00	0-679-74596-3
____ **The Man Who Went Up in Smoke** by Maj Sjöwall and Per Wahlöö	$9.00	0-679-74597-1
____ **Roseanna** by Maj Sjöwall and Per Wahlöö	$9.00	0-679-74598-X
____ **After Dark, My Sweet** by Jim Thompson	$7.95	0-679-73247-0
____ **The Alcoholics** by Jim Thompson	$8.00	0-679-73313-2
____ **The Criminal** by Jim Thompson	$8.00	0-679-73314-0
____ **Cropper's Cabin** by Jim Thompson	$8.00	0-679-73315-9
____ **The Getaway** by Jim Thompson	$8.95	0-679-73250-0
____ **The Grifters** by Jim Thompson	$8.95	0-679-73248-9
____ **A Hell of a Woman** by Jim Thompson	$10.00	0-679-73251-9
____ **The Killer Inside Me** by Jim Thompson	$9.00	0-679-73397-3
____ **Nothing More Than Murder** by Jim Thompson	$9.00	0-679-73309-4
____ **Pop. 1280** by Jim Thompson	$9.00	0-679-73249-7
____ **Recoil** by Jim Thompson	$8.00	0-679-73308-6
____ **Savage Night** by Jim Thompson	$8.00	0-679-73310-8
____ **A Swell-Looking Babe** by Jim Thompson	$8.00	0-679-73311-6
____ **Wild Town** by Jim Thompson	$9.00	0-679-73312-4
____ **Web of Murder** by Harry Whittington	$9.00	0-679-74068-6
____ **The Burnt Orange Heresy** by Charles Willeford	$7.95	0-679-73252-7
____ **Cockfighter** by Charles Willeford	$9.00	0-679-73471-6
____ **Pick-Up** by Charles Willeford	$7.95	0-679-73253-5
____ **The Hot Spot** by Charles Williams	$8.95	0-679-73329-9

Available at your bookstore or call toll-free to order: 1-800-733-3000.
Credit cards only. Prices subject to change.